He joined his lips with hers, fiercely at first, but then they softened. Selina was floating, floating in his arms while the hay swirled about them. Then, with a start, she realized she truly was suspended for he had swooped her up off the floor.

He laid her down in a soft stack of hay, then came to rest beside her, one leg crossed with hers.

"Selina . . ." He breathed her name like some sort of prayer. "Selina, you've been so hard to resist."

Joy shot through her on a trembling wave, cresting near her lips. She wanted to cry out with the pleasure his hands were working. . . .

By Patricia Wynn
Published by Fawcett Books:

THE BUMBLEBROTH
A COUNTRY AFFAIR

A
COUNTRY
AFFAIR

Patricia Wynn

FAWCETT CREST • NEW YORK

A Fawcett Crest Book
Published by Ballantine Books
Copyright © 1996 by Patricia Wynn Ricks

http://www.randomhouse.com

Library of Congress Catalog Card Number: 95-96179

ISBN: 0-449-22402-3

Manufactured in the United States of America

First Edition: July 1996

10   9   8   7   6   5   4   3   2   1

To my valentine,
From his old farm-girl

Chapter One

November 1813

The house had long been abed, when Selina, wrapped in a moth-eaten coverlet, made her way down the creaking, darkened stairs. Weary as she was from a long day of work, she could not rest until she had written the letter.

She stoked the kitchen fire, adding logs to get a good flame going and warming her frozen fingertips, before lighting a tallow candle. Moving to the chest that housed her mother's few treasured possessions, she sorted through its papers until she found the valentine.

Its silvered edges had been torn and frayed. The ink was faded in places, and the paper yellowed. But the words of its message could still clearly be read.

Selina carried it to the table and propped it up against a stack of books where she could see it while she wrote. Before beginning, she placed the candle at a distance so its sputtering would not burn her sheet of paper. Then, with a sigh, she took a seat and dipped her quill in ink.

Memories of her father, and what he would say if he knew what she was about to do, made her pause. A wave of shame washed through her. But the vicar had convinced her. She had no other choice, and her brother understood.

"This is for him," Selina whispered, hoping her father's

spirit would forgive her, as she scratched her first words on the page.

"What the—"

Richard Trevelyan stared at the letter he had just opened and muttered a curse before perusing it again. It was dated as having been written on the fifth of January 1814, and it bore the seal of the College of Arms.

To the Right Honorable the Earl of Linton

My Lord,

I deem it proper to acquaint you that an application has recently been made to the College by Mr. Augustus Payley, Esq., of Uckfield in Sussex, for a Warrant which would enable him to take the ancient Surname of Trevelyan and to bear its arms.

However, no proofs have been exhibited to me relative to the connection of the said Family of Trevelyan and Augustus Payley, nor have I found that his ancestors have ever used the name. Upon examination, I have discovered him to be a Husbandman with no Pedigree to manifest the right of any of his descendants to the Trevelyan Armorial bearings.

In some cases, the proof of long usage coupled with a very great probability of a connection has afforded grounds for the allowance of Arms so used. But, in the case in question, I have found it my duty to withhold my assent.

In making this communication to you, for your own private information, I trust you will consider the Garter of the present day fully desirous to preserve the integrity of the ancient and respectable Families. . . .

Richard skimmed the last paragraph and noted the signature at the bottom: Isaac Heard, Garter King of Arms.

"Devil take the mushroom!" Richard swore again. But the violence of his own reaction made him pause. It was not often that a matter so trivial as a spurious claim to his name would anger him so.

As he reflected, however, upon the duty that faced him this morning, he discovered there might be a cause for his unreasonable fury.

It was Wilfrid, of course. Why Richard had been cursed with the greatest rakeshame in London for his heir, he did not know. But the fact was, Sir Wilfrid Bart was one of the most reprehensible men Richard had ever had the pleasure to know, and at this particular moment, he had reached the limit of his tolerance for him.

Wilfrid was due to call at any minute to receive another in a long history of well-deserved tongue-lashings. Richard had learned that Wilfrid had been trading upon his expectations again, and to such an extent that his newest debts must surely amount into the thousands of pounds. Since Wilfrid had no hope of ever paying these off unless Richard died, the earl was understandably vexed.

He had no intention of ever obliging his older cousin. Strong and healthy, and, at thirty, in the prime of his manhood, Richard felt no worries on the subject of his continued existence. All he needed to do, he comforted himself, was to marry and produce a legion of sons in order to cut Wilfrid out of the succession.

The fact that he had not yet done so did not mean he intended to relinquish the right. But he had to admit that finding a suitable wife—one he could imagine sharing his life with for over two weeks running—seemed more difficult with each passing year. At the moment he was so incensed with Wilfrid as to contemplate picking the next girl he saw just to see Wilfrid's face when he announced his upcoming nuptials.

But, Richard reflected ruefully, Wilfrid was of such an optimistically avaricious disposition, he would likely refuse to believe that a loss to himself was possible until Richard had kicked up his toes, and the money and title had been bestowed upon someone else.

And even then Wilfrid would count the heirs between himself and the succession, and simply recalculate his odds.

When Richard's butler opened the library door to announce the arrival of Sir Wilfrid Bart, Richard was still clutching the Garter's letter in his hand. He laid it open upon his desk, reflecting that now he had another leech in Wilfrid's mold to contend with.

By the time his cousin entered, Richard had seated himself on the other side of the desk. He did not rise to greet Wilfrid even though the temptation to loom over him was almost irresistible.

"Cousin?" A rouged and powdered dandy of some fifty years peered anxiously into the room and forced a smile. Wilfrid's hesitant entry, as always, afforded Richard some degree of amusement until he reminded himself that this man was his heir. "I believe you expressed a desire to see me?" Wilfrid said.

He assumed an expression of complete innocence, a pose that was belied by his defensive hunch of one shoulder and the halting steps he used to approach the desk.

Today Richard found he could not laugh at the sight of this cringing posture. The letter had loosed his temper, when he preferred to make a practice of holding it in check. He endeavored to do so now, before speaking.

His delay only served to make Wilfrid more uneasy. Wilfrid smiled, then tittered. "I say, cuz, do you mean to offer me a chair?"

"By all means." Richard indicated the seat across from him. "You must make yourself comfortable."

Before Wilfrid could relax too much at this polite treatment, however, Richard added, "I do not expect you will feel so for long."

Wilfrid started. He had seated himself at right angles to the desk, as if unable to meet his cousin's gaze, and now the tip of his high shirt point caught him in the eye.

He tittered again. "My word, cuz, how you do give a fellow a fright. I believe you delight in it."

For a brief moment, Richard thought he caught a gleam of hatred in Wilfrid's eyes. But if he did, it was quickly masked by Wilfrid's normal vacant look. Richard shrugged off the possibility. If Wilfrid resented him, it would be quite natural, and Richard was too sure of his position to let a coward's hatred concern him.

"It seems," he began instead, "that I shall soon have reason to offer you my condolences."

Wilfrid paled, and Richard smiled sweetly.

"Condolences?" Wilfrid's tongue swept his lips. "What condolences would those be, cousin?"

"I understand you anticipate some bereavement? An impending death in the family? Or so I hear."

Wilfrid's color returned, and Richard realized that he had been thinking of something else. Perhaps that his cousin, the earl, might have decided to marry after all.

"I am afraid I do not follow you, cousin."

"Come, come, now, Wilfrid," Richard chided him. "Do I really strike you as so decrepit? Have I not done my share of boxing and riding to hounds? But perhaps you do not consider those healthful pursuits?"

Wilfrid smiled nervously, but he was undefeated. "I perceive you were making a joke, dear boy. Always one for a laugh, even as an adorable child."

"This is no joking matter, Wilfrid. I have no plans to

stick my spoon into the wall just to please you, and so I warn you."

"Warn me? Now, cousin. Why should you feel the need to warn me?"

"Because I have been privileged to receive complaints from the tradesmen you have abused in my name. A name that means a great deal to me." Surprised again by his own vehemence, Richard cast a glance at the letter facing Wilfrid, wishing he could permanently be relieved of this sort of worry.

Wilfrid followed his glance. After a moment's look at the paper, he turned his own pale face back to Richard's. "But, cuz, you do not mean you have listened to some worthless scoundrel's lies. They are all lies, I tell you!"

Richard reached into the drawer. "Are these all lies?" He flung a stack of IOUs over the desktop. They scattered, covering up his own papers.

With trembling hands, Wilfrid scooped up the strewn vouchers and, for a few seconds, tried to pretend he had never seen them by studying them intently. This was only to buy time, Richard knew, and for once that day, he did want to laugh. His elderly cousin must certainly take the prize for gall. Richard was truly surprised that Wilfrid should try such a foolish tactic, and especially for so long.

Wilfrid certainly was not relishing the prospect of having to own up to his vowels, for his skin looked clammy and his fingers were still trembling.

Before Richard could grow impatient, however, Wilfrid stopped reading and looked up, a certain tension in his pose.

"I cannot see that this letter has anything to do with me," he said.

"Let me see." Richard frowned and reached out one hand. The paper Wilfrid placed in it was the letter from the Garter King of Arms.

"No, you are correct, Wilfrid. This one has nothing to do with you, though I do see a point of resemblance that would certainly fail to amuse you, so I will not share it. You must have picked it up with the others."

"When did it come?"

"This morning. I was just reading it when you arrived."

Thinking, apparently, that he had diverted Richard's attention from himself, Wilfrid relaxed. "The fool," he scoffed. "Did he think to become one of us, just by asking?"

One of us? Wilfrid's assumption of affinity with him roused Richard's ire as nothing else had that morning. He would be damned if he would be considered as forming some sort of pack with Wilfrid Bart.

Something else in Wilfrid's tone, however, caused him to say, "A fool? Why? Do you know him?"

Wilfrid started. "Me? Of course not. How should I know a mere farmer? I was only commenting upon the absurdity of his claim."

"The name Payley means nothing to you?"

"Nothing at all. One knows Payleys, I suppose, the way one knows Smiths, but I have never been acquainted with an Augustus Payley." Richard could see Wilfrid was telling the truth.

"I see. Perhaps, however, we should get back to our original topic, which, as I recall, had to do with some claims you yourself have made."

Wilfrid assumed a look of bonhomie. "My dear Richard, even you must know that one is forced on occasion to stretch the truth to be able to live properly as a gentleman. I could not possibly begin to keep up with the Carlton House set if I did not borrow money. And since you are my only recourse, I am naturally compelled to use your name. Everyone does something of the sort. I

7

daresay Prinny himself has borrowed in excess, if you consider how he builds whole palaces upon credit and waits for the notes to come in."

"Are you saying the allowance I pay you is insufficient to support a gentleman?"

Wilfrid's eyes shifted. Richard could see he was weighing the consequences of insulting his sole means of support in favor of the chance that his allowance might be increased. Richard, however, did not feel up to playing with his heir any longer, and his countenance must have reflected this, for Wilfrid gave up at once.

"Of course not, cuz. You are far, far too generous."

"I am not asking for compliments, Wilfrid. I want to know how you explain the borrowing of thousands of pounds."

Wilfrid shrugged, and again that hint of hostility showed in his glance. "I wish I could explain it, dear Richard, but there it is. When Prinny beckons, I must go. He finds me vastly amusing, and I must say I do enjoy palace life."

"Then, I suggest you try enjoying it less. I do not mean to pay these vouchers, and if I do not, there will be no choice for you but to run to the Continent.

"And," Richard continued, smiling amicably, even though his teeth were clenched, "if you continue to be-smirch my name or to use it improperly, I just might send you there myself."

"It is all very well for you!" Wilfrid started up in his chair. "You, who were fortunate enough to be born to the title!"

"You were born to a title, too. Have you forgotten you're a baronet?"

Wilfrid's expression turned bitter. "How could I forget my miserable inheritance when the fellows are forever making jokes upon my name? 'Always a Bart, and never a peer.' Most amusing, don't you think?"

Richard did smile. Wilfrid's gall, his unbridled ambition and greed—when anyone else would have been satisfied with his rank—never failed to leave him laughing.

"My heart bleeds for you, cousin. But I do have a word of advice. If your aspirations to be a peer are so formidable, you might think of trying to earn a peerage. There ought to be room for a gentleman of your caliber in the army, and—*damned*, if I wouldn't be happy to purchase you a pair of colors myself."

Richard's offer failed to brighten Wilfrid's hopes. "Don't be ridiculous, cousin," he said, wrinkling his nose. "Even if I had a mind for the army—and the very thought of it makes me shudder—the army would never consider a man of my age and noted infirmities."

"Infirmities? If you are so infirm, Wilfrid, I am astonished at the hours you keep."

Wilfrid smiled smoothly. "But I keep telling you, Richard. I cannot refuse Prinny anything. Why, even now, he has need of my company in Brighton."

"Brighton in the winter?" Richard shook his head. "You astonish me, Wilfrid."

"But he does, dear boy. Something about a new wing. Seeking a diversion, I suspect. Still torn up about Brummell, don't you know."

"The Regent's feelings do not concern me at the moment. I would be far more interested to hear what you intend doing about these debts."

"Doing?" Wilfrid blinked. "I do not see that I can afford to do anything about them, if you do not mean to pay them."

"You can hardly afford to do nothing. Have you given any thought to employment?"

"I—?" Wilfrid's expression suggested that Richard

had made the cleverest joke imaginable. "Dear boy. There is no employment on earth, at least to my knowledge, that would contrive to pay such a mountain of debts."

Richard leaned back in his chair and let his gaze sweep Wilfrid from his pomaded locks to the tips of his tasseled boots. "You might reflect upon that fact, dear cuz," he said in biting accents, "when next you sit down to the card table. Or when you next place an order to your wine merchant."

Wilfrid could not fail to appreciate the searing tone of Richard's voice, and even he appeared somewhat contrite. "Certainly, cousin, if you wish it, I shall reflect upon those points."

"And you will oblige me by not insinuating again that I am at death's door."

"You exaggerate. I am certain I never used those precise words."

"Near enough as makes no difference." Richard stood. "And now, dear cousin, I believe I have enjoyed your company enough for one day."

As Wilfrid stood, his smile of farewell did not reach his eyes, and Richard perceived that his words would have no lasting effect upon his cousin's comportment.

At least he thought not. But then Wilfrid turned at the door with a serious look.

"Before I forget, cuz. What do you mean to do about that upstart Payley? Ignore him, I hope?"

Richard started to agree, but then he paused. The letter still rankled. He had received no satisfaction from Wilfrid, and his temper had not been appeased. It was bad enough to have one scoundrel abusing his name without another one added.

"I suppose," he said, silently proposing a journey to himself, "that I shall have to look into the matter."

Wilfrid laughed, but his laughter had an edge to it. "Oh, surely, cousin, you do not think there is any merit in his claim?"

"Of course I do not. But I think Mr. Augustus Payley should be spoken to for his presumption."

"Then, let me speak to him," Wilfrid surprised him by saying. "Uckfield is on the way down to Brighton, or so I believe. I should be most happy to perform this commission for you."

Wilfrid's offer had been made so quickly as to sound sincere, but Richard reflected that his cousin might be hoping for some sort of reprieve—a loan perhaps, or even a payment of his debts, if he rendered Richard this service.

"No thank you, Wilfrid. I think I shall handle this situation myself. I seem to be rather in the mood to demand satisfaction."

"Plan on calling him out?" A gleam lit Wilfrid's eye.

"Call out a farmer? Not . . . *one of us*?" Richard stressed. "You must be joking, Wilfrid. And, here, I had been thinking you had not been blessed with a sense of humor.

"No," Richard continued, thinking aloud, "I simply mean to confront this Augustus Payley and rid him of the idea that he can use my name at will."

Wilfrid seemed reluctant to leave the matter at that. "Then, I hope you mean to teach him a serious lesson. And, if I may be of any help whatsoever, I beg you will write to me in Brighton."

"Certainly, I shall. I could not forget the depth of your family feeling."

A glint hardened Wilfrid's eyes. "Do not underestimate it, Richard. My little foibles are as nothing when compared to this gross encroachment. I beg again that you will let me tend to it."

Taken aback by the strength of Wilfrid's feelings, Richard moderated his tone. "I appreciate your interest, but your methods are not likely to be the same as mine, so I prefer to see to this myself."

His offer having been so firmly refused, Wilfrid shrugged. "As you will. Your servant, cousin."

As Wilfrid showed himself out, Richard stared after him, and a rare feeling of dismay swept through him. Wilfrid had left, not the least bit abashed. Richard had no doubt that his cousin would take up where he had left off with no change at all in his behavior.

And it did not matter that he was regarded by most to be a thoroughly undeserving character. Richard was obliged to support him. A gentleman was frowned upon for mistreating his heir, and, in truth, Wilfrid did nothing worse than many of his contemporaries. If the Regent himself found Wilfrid charming—and Richard scoffed at the thought—what could he do to make him feel otherwise?

The source of his dismay, he knew, was the niggling thought that Wilfrid just might succeed him if he failed to provide another heir. Men Richard's age died all the time, and many an elderly man had succeeded a younger one. In spite of his good health, Richard knew he could break his neck on a hunt or in a carriage race, whereas Wilfrid took great care never to court any physical danger.

What was needed was a wife. Richard admitted to himself that his search for one had grown more serious of late. The need to supplant Wilfrid was always in his mind, but an even stronger motive, he realized, was his more recent desire for companionship. A man grew weary of nothing but frivolous pursuits once the first energy of his youth had been spent. The trouble was, the longer he looked for his ideal companion, the more unlikely it appeared that he would find her.

The fresh, young faces that were trotted out every social season were looking more and more the same. Richard thought that if he had to attend one more ball, he might take to serious drink.

The letter in his hand caught Richard's attention once again, bringing with it a new wave of irritation. *And now this Payley scoundrel.* His family obligations were enough to send even the most cheerful fellow into the dismals.

The thought of facing Payley down cheered Richard immensely. If nothing else, a trip into Sussex would get him out of London. He had a mind to ride his horse all the way to Uckfield in spite of the winter season, leaving his coach and servants behind.

A rigorous journey on horseback would be the very thing he needed to cure him of his malaise.

Chapter Two

*B*risk, cold weather and the sight of open country-side—however bleak and leafless it was—did restore Richard to his normal equanimity. He had left London behind with all its tedious formalities. Even his change in dress came as a relief, for one could not go jaunting about the countryside in January dressed like a pink of the ton. His woolen breeches, waistcoat, and jacket made him feel more the country gentleman, and only the mag-nificent cut of his caped redingote divulged the class of its wearer.

He left well before dawn, and a brisk day of traveling brought him to Uckfield in time for dinner. Uckfield proved to be a small hamlet of little distinction, due with-out doubt to its distance from the turnpike road. By the time Richard arrived, he was ready for a warm drink even though the ocean currents that warmed Sussex had kept his fingers and toes from freezing.

He headed for the inn, a modest place unused to the carriage trade by the looks of it, where he found he had to stable his own horse. Unable to locate a blanket, he threw his redingote over the beast. Emerging from the stable a few minutes later, he had to dodge a pair of boys and their dog, who had started a footrace in the yard.

The innkeeper soon had Richard ensconced in his tap-room by the fire, since no private parlors were to be had in such a small establishment. The inn was poor, but the owner, Mr. Croft, seemed a respectable sort of fellow. And Richard could be satisfied not only with his dinner, but also with the rum punch the man concocted at an hour when most of his customers would normally be tending their livestock.

Richard waited until the rum had seeped into his bones and warmed him from the inside out before inquiring where he might find Mr. Augustus Payley, Esq.

"Ye want the squire?" the good-natured Mr. Croft asked, obviously surprised.

"If that is how Mr. Payley is known hereabouts."

Richard had replied in a voice that said he was not used to having his wishes questioned. Then, relaxing, he reasoned in all fairness that he had not given Mr. Croft his name or his rank.

The innkeeper laughed on an apologetic note. "Sorry, sir. It's just that ye fair took me aback, askin' about our squire in that sort o' way."

Something about the manner in which Mr. Croft had said "our squire" struck Richard as odd. But before he could ask why his query had astonished his host, Mr. Croft continued.

"I can direct ye to him all right. If ye want to follow me this way." The burly man set down the cloth he had been using to polish his tables and led Richard to a small window at the front of the inn.

"There be the squire," he said, pointing out into his yard.

Richard had to bend nearly in half to see through the low glass, and when he did, he saw nothing but the two boys and a dog, who by this time had finished their race. Now they were engaged in a spirited game of tag instead, with the spaniel an energetic third player.

Richard looked about for a gentleman. Then the earlier

note in the innkeeper's voice recurred to him, and he thought he knew why the man had used it.

"Would Mr. Augustus Payley be one of those two young scamps?" he asked.

Mr. Croft laughed. "Aye, sir. Now ye see why ye confounded me for a moment. Ye sounded so formal-like. Ay—" he made a gesture toward the boys, which, though amused, contained a measure of pride as well—"that be our squire. He be ten years old, or thereabouts."

"Which of the two is he?"

Mr. Croft's honest face displayed shock at Richard's failure to recognize quality when he saw it. "Oh, that be plain as day, sir. That littler boy, now, the one with the red muffler, that be my son, Johnny. 'Tis the other one be the squire."

It was clear that the very idea of confusing the two boys had greatly discomfited Mr. Croft, but indeed, there was little to choose between them. Both were dressed in baggy, woolen breeches and knitted waistcoats, beneath which rough-looking linen showed. The only distinguishing marks between them were the color of the mufflers wound about their necks and, perhaps, the degree of blondness exhibited by each. Mr. Croft's Johnny was a towhead, where Augustus's hair already displayed a tendency to turn brown.

For a moment, Richard watched the two cavorting outside, wondering on what sort of fool's errand he had come. If the squire was ten years old, then who had written the application?

Mr. Croft had gone back to polishing his tables in preparation for his evening customers. Richard thought of asking for more particulars about the Payleys, then decided against this course. Where family matters were concerned, the fewer outsiders involved the better, and until he knew who had been using a boy to cover his own nefarious dealings, Richard would rather keep the news to himself. Something fairly havey-cavey seemed to be going on.

Meaning to question the boy, he bent to look outside the window again, but the squire had disappeared. The innkeeper's Johnny had fetched an ax to split some logs.

"Your squire appears to have decamped," Richard remarked idly to his host.

Mr. Croft checked his timepiece. "Yessir. It'll be time for milking up at the Grange, and Mr. Augustus be a good one for remembering his chores."

"Is he now? And the Grange, I take it, is the Payley estate?"

Mr. Croft confirmed this and, after giving Richard directions to the Grange, agreed to his borrowing a gig while his own horse rested.

With Johnny's help, the gig was readied, and Richard soon found himself urging the inn's one horse up a road deeply rutted by cart wheels. Lurching and bumping with each rut, he reached the crest of a short hill and immediately spotted Augustus trudging homeward. The boy, who appeared to be in a vast hurry, was stumbling over the ruts in his haste.

Richard lightly flicked the horse on the back with the reins and, in spite of the dismal road, soon overtook him.

"May I offer you a ride?" Richard asked as soon as the boy turned to see who could be passing him.

"Yessir! Thank you, sir!"

Wreathed in smiles, Augustus clambered up onto the seat beside him. His head was bare, and the winter's setting sun sparkled in his blond highlights.

If Richard had not been on guard, he would have been disarmed by the boy's frank gratitude. As it was, he had to fight a strong urge to smile back at him.

"Have you far to go?" Richard asked, clicking to the

horse, though the innkeeper had already told him the distance to the Grange.

"No, it's not much farther. Just another mile up this road. I walk it all the time, but I left a little later than I should have, which makes me doubly glad you came along when you did, sir."

They bucked for a moment in silence.

"And whom do I have the pleasure of conveying?"

Augustus flushed and bobbed his head in the best bow he could manage under the perilous circumstances. "Your pardon, sir, I ought to have introduced myself. Augustus Payley, Esquire, at your service."

Richard offered the boy his hand and was pleased by the firmness of his handshake. "Your servant, Mr. Payley." He hoped Augustus would not notice his failure to identify himself, but Richard knew he would be unlikely to get much information from the boy if he did.

"Were you heading for the Grange yourself?"

Startled by the question, Richard hesitated before responding, "As a matter of fact, I was. How did you know?"

Augustus chuckled. "Excuse me, sir, but you almost had to be. We have the only farm up this road, and besides, we've been expecting you."

"I see." So far the day had been full of surprises, none of which had helped Richard at all.

"Yessir. We thought you might come yesterday, but when you did not, we thought you might have been taken ill."

And who is we? Richard had started to phrase this question more politely aloud when Augustus said, "Pardon me, sir, but it might be better for me to lead your horse down this hill." Without waiting for Richard's agreement, he jumped down from the gig.

Richard, who was not used to needing his horses led,

was completely taken aback until he saw the reason for the boy's action. A rut, deeper and wider than all the others, had made the next descent more than uncomfortable. It would be an easy matter to trap a wheel and overturn the gig while trying to pull it out.

Richard had no doubt of his ability to guide the horse around it, but he let the boy do as he wished. This Augustus Payley, whoever he was, certainly had an engaging way about him.

The hill once negotiated, Augustus scrambled back onto the seat. Richard thanked him kindly for his service and took control of the horse again.

"We're coming to the Grange now, sir. Do you see our orchard?"

Noting the pride in the boy's voice, Richard followed his gesture to see that, indeed, they were about to pass an immense orchard, filled with dormant cherry trees. Grass had been left to grow thick around their bases, but it had been beaten down and grazed by a large number of sheep.

"You ought to see the cherries we harvested last season," Augustus said. "For size and sweetness, I'd put them up against any fruit from Kent."

Distracted by the thought of how lovely the trees would appear in their spring blossoms, Richard delayed his questions once again. But his curiosity was growing: about this boy, who seemed somewhat mature for his age, and about the person who was raising him. Augustus had the courtesy of a gentleman, the pride of a landed farmer, and the engaging manner of the best of his age and gender. Reflecting upon his anger at the start of this adventure, Richard almost regretted the errand he had come upon.

He opened his mouth to question the boy more firmly, but was suddenly interrupted by a cry.

"Oh! Lord love me! He's at it again!"

"He—" Richard turned to spy another, smaller orchard, this one full of young sprigs planted in close rows.

A large bull was making his way slowly through them, stopping only to nibble the top off every one.

Without waiting for the carriage to stop, Augustus jumped down from the seat and started to run.

"Here! Augustus, where are you going?"

"Got to get Caesar out of m'sister's garden. Sorry, sir!" He struggled over the fence that should have shielded the young plants, shouting and waving his arms at the bull.

Knowing the squire would be too busy to direct him farther, Richard smiled after him, before looking about for the house. It was perched upon a hill just past the smaller orchard and a tumbledown barn. The yard appeared to be a gathering place for wretched outbuildings and decayed machinery.

As soon as he reached the door of the Grange, Richard stepped down and looked about for a servant to take his horse, but the dilapidated condition of the house suggested no servant would appear. Seeing none in any case, he knocked upon the ancient door, which needed a new coat of paint, but to no reply.

Curious, and growing more so at the silence of the place, he decided to stable the horse himself. He did not want the beast to take a chill while waiting.

The ramshackle barn was only a few paces away. Richard unharnessed the mare and led her into it, ducking to avoid hitting his head on the sagging door frame. As his eyes grew accustomed to the dimmer light, the odor of sweet hay and warm farm animals assaulted his nostrils.

"Clarissa"—a feminine voice came from the other side of a stall—"if you don't stop this at once, I shall be forced to call Mr. Dowling, who will take you away. He has been dying to get his hands upon you."

Wondering what poor Clarissa had done to merit such a threat, Richard tied Mr. Croft's horse and peered over the wooden slats.

A particularly pretty Jersey cow greeted his eyes. She was gazing soulfully at a maid who was milking her, and, with an inward chuckle, Richard guessed that Mr. Dowling must be the local gluemaker.

The maid herself was partially out of his line of sight, her back turned toward Richard, so that he had to advance another step past the stall to see her.

When he did, what struck him first was the glossiness of her hair, which tumbled down her back in a thick fall of brown silk. Its rich, dark color was brightened by hints of auburn and ebony. The mass screened her shoulders and back, so that it was a few seconds before he remarked her height, which seemed considerable.

Her perfect proportions—a narrow waist above a voluminous skirt that was much too heavy to be fashionable—had also concealed this detail from him. But the girl sitting in front of him, he realized, would surely be tall enough to meet his eyes if she stood.

The cow stomped, and the bucket beneath its udder threatened to topple over.

"Clarissa!" Again, a sharp note of warning. "I have no time for this foolishness. If you do not behave, I swear I shall let Caesar have his way with you."

Restraining a smile, and convinced now that this milkmaid was no servant—not with the cultured voice she had used—Richard judged it was time to reveal himself before she could swear in earnest. He felt the need, besides, to see the face that went with that hair and waist.

"Herrrumph!" He cleared his throat discreetly, and the girl turned without jumping, as he had feared she might.

Vibrant eyes, warm in color, high cheekbones, and an open stare met his gaze. Richard felt a strange thump in the region of his chest.

The girl had recognized him as a stranger, but instead of blushing for her conduct, she rose with a flashing white smile.

Richard had been right: the girl reached clear to his shoulder and beyond. As a man who measured over six feet, he was not used to looking many men in the eye, and never a woman. He found the experience had an unusual effect. He could only stare in rapt admiration of her magnificent proportions: from her full, rounded breasts, to her high waist, to what, beneath her skirts, must be very long legs.

She seemed momentarily to be struck by the strangeness of the phenomenon herself as her eyes raked him from his boots to the top of his head.

Aware of the impropriety of his manners, and puzzling over his heart, which was still beating erratically, Richard cleared his throat again. "Pardon me, miss, but I knocked at the door and no one answered."

"No, I am sorry." She advanced and offered him her hand with the same open manner Augustus had shown. "I did not hear you arrive, and I'm afraid you saw how I was occupied." She made a disparaging gesture toward the miscreant she had been trying to milk. "My brother should have returned from the village in time to do the milking, but since he did not, I decided to begin. Clarissa's mooing can be quite disturbing."

"I do understand that a lady in her condition must not be kept waiting."

In response to these words, the girl—whoever she was—did flush becomingly and as if she had never done so before. Richard took a momentary pleasure in the way embarrassment brought a warm glow to her cheeks, before the thumping, moving lower than his chest, warned him of the danger of flirting with pretty milking maids, whether servants or no.

Considering the crudity of their surroundings, he only doffed his hat as he asked for her name, "Miss . . . ?"

His single word erased her embarrassment, and she bobbed him a brisk curtsy. "Selina—" She hesitated only a second, before continuing more boldly, "Miss Selina Trevelyan, sir. And you must be . . . ?"

Her use of his family name shocked Richard. His brows snapped together before he vouchsafed to answer. Wondering briefly whether his title would wipe the brave look from her face, he made her a stiffer bow and began, "I am Linton—" before he was cut off by a bovine bellow.

"Caesar! Oh, the devil!"

Taken aback by her oath, Richard suppressed a grin as she flew past him. Compared to the restrained "luds" of ladies of the ton, her spirit was refreshing. Miss Trevelyan—he assumed, Miss Payley—had bolted from the barn as fast as her brother had escaped the gig.

Richard followed her.

The bull, it appeared, had refused to be herded, and was still making short shrift of the sprouted trees. Augustus had stopped his waving in favor of beating the bull with a stout stick, which, though inadequate for what he wanted, had resulted in Caesar's bellow.

"Caesar, I will kill you and roast you for pudding!"

A smile that had begun to tease Richard's mouth at Selina's admonishment quickly faded when he saw how truly distressed she was. Not in the least frightened of the beast, she climbed through the fence and ran after him. She snatched the switch from Augustus's hand and laid into the bull, tears just below the surface of her fury.

Richard hastily looked around and spied a nearby

haystack from which to borrow a fistful of hay. With his long legs he took the fence in little more than a second. Then, reaching the bull, he stretched out his offering.

Caesar took one whiff of the sweet-smelling hay and was instantly distracted from the seedlings, which must have tasted bitter in comparison. As Richard retreated toward the opening in the fence, Caesar followed with his waddling gait.

"Oh, thank you, Mr. Lint!"

Startled by the unfamiliar name, Richard remembered that his introduction had been cut off as he was giving his title. Selina must have heard only its first syllable.

"I ought to have thought of hay myself," she said, coming around the other side of the bull, "but I'm afraid my temper got the best of me."

"Perfectly understandable, I am sure." Richard handed her the hay bouquet, and Caesar's nose followed with it. "Under these circumstances, one feels much better for the chance to give one or two serious thwacks."

In proof of this statement, Augustus was still following them and applying the ineffectual stick at every other step.

Richard added, "Besides, Caesar certainly deserved a beating."

"Did he not?"

Selina's sigh pulled at Richard's heart. Judging by the time Caesar had been loose among the trees, Richard knew that many had been killed. He did not need to see the poor condition of the fence, the run-down house, or the crumbling barn to know the Payleys could ill afford such a loss.

And where were the other Payleys? So far, Richard had seen only the two, when clearly there must be more. He supposed they must have gone to market in another village or to make some calls.

"It looks as though someone will have to repair that fence," he said, noticing where the bull had broken in.

"Yes, I—that is, someone will this evening."

Selina's slip of the tongue jolted him from his comfort. "Do you not have anyone in your employ to do the job?" he asked, suspecting he knew the answer already.

"I am afraid not." Selina's tone was light. "But it's no matter. I have done such things before."

"You shouldn't be—"

A proud lifting of her chin warned him not to protest. Richard broke off before he could embarrass her again.

But—Confound it! he thought. Were all her people invalid that she should take this upon herself? He could not let a lady—for she *was* a lady, despite her use of strong expressions—he could never permit her to perform such a task.

"I could fix that fence for you in a trice," he said, wondering at the speed with which he'd made the offer.

If any other man had been around, Richard would immediately have paid him to do the work. Richard himself had not done anything of the kind in years. But his father had been of the opinion that an aristocrat should know all about the workings of his estates and, consequently, had made certain his son knew at least the rudiments of carpentry and farming. Richard had enjoyed that part of his training.

"Oh, I could not ask you—"

"You did not ask me, Miss—Trevelyan." Richard caught himself before addressing her as Payley. Now did not seem the proper time to straighten out the matter.

Dark was coming, and if the fence was to be mended today, it would have to be done at once before Clarissa decided to follow Caesar's example. Richard had noticed the missing pieces to the barn's walls. It would be a small matter for the bull to break through again.

"But—" Selina, it seemed, was not used to accepting anyone's help. "I could not abuse your time so. Haven't you come about the trees?"

Trees? Richard supposed she must have been expecting a nurseryman, the same person Augustus had mistaken him for.

"I have come about trees," he agreed cautiously. Family trees, he said truthfully to himself. He was not about to reveal his identity until the fence was mended. If Selina knew for one second the errand he had come upon, she would never allow him to help her, and Richard discovered he wanted to do this much.

He reasoned that whoever had made the application for his name, this girl needed all the help she could get. He had noticed the roughness of her hand and knew that work had produced that roughness. At the moment, in spite of her vibrant coloring, she looked about to drop.

"The trees can wait until tomorrow," Richard said. He figured he could put up at Mr. Croft's inn, which had seemed pleasant and clean enough.

"But won't your employer complain if you are detained?"

He could not miss the anxiety in her voice. Richard wondered just exactly what their anticipated visitor had been expected to accomplish. It was quite possible that the man would show up tomorrow, but until he did, and as long as Richard did not lie to her, precisely, he told himself he had nothing to worry about.

"I have all the time I need" was all he said on that subject. "And, besides, it seems I must wait anyway for the gentleman with whom I am to conduct my business."

At this, instead of telling him when he might expect to see the gentleman in charge, Selina drew herself up. "You will have to conduct your business with me, sir. You see"—she beckoned Augustus forward, and the boy made Richard a low bow—"this is Mr. Augustus Trevelyan, Esquire, and I, as his sole living relative, represent him."

"Do you?" Richard's rhetorical question conveyed none of his shock at her pronouncement. This investigation was becoming more intriguing with each passing moment. Selina, then, must have been the person who wrote the letter of application, though why a boy's sister should do such a thing he could not imagine. And were there really no more members of this household?

Richard found himself fascinated by the mystery.

"Well, Miss Tr—" He could not bring himself to call her Trevelyan again, not when she had used his name without permission. "We shall have plenty of time tomorrow, I trust, to carry out our business."

His tone must have conveyed its usual authority, for Selina nodded and said, "Augustus, why don't you help Mr. Lint and bring him all he needs to fix the fence while I attend to our supper?"

Richard winced at her mistaking his name. He was not used to practicing deception, but at the moment he saw no way out of this. Tomorrow, he trusted, would be soon enough to rectify it.

Augustus agreed cheerily and ran into the barn to fetch some tools. Selina curtsied again, and Richard admired the straightness of her back.

Tired with work she might be, and disappointed, but still she carried herself like a lady. Her graceful curtsy had been worthy of a presentation gown. Her shoulders were elegant though broad, and the dress she wore hugged them tightly, showing off their alluring curvature. But Selina seemed oblivious to her charms as she excused herself.

Richard watched her move toward the house and had to admit the view was just as good from this side: the way she walked with her head held high, the slight swing of her hips beneath her tattered gown, and her narrow waist just beneath the luxuriant fall of hair.

He had to admit that the girl had pluck, too. He almost regretted his errand now. He would not enjoy embarrassing, perhaps even arguing with, a girl who needed his help.

And who did not like to accept it.

Remembering how she had reacted to his offer, Richard decided he had best get to work before Selina changed her mind and sent him packing before he could fix the fence. He removed his woolen jacket and rolled up his sleeves.

Chapter Three

 *F*eeling relieved of a burden, which for her was a rare sensation, Selina was halfway to the kitchen before she remembered Clarissa and the milk. The cow could not be left so swollen, or the milk left to sour in the bucket. Since Augustus was busy helping the stranger, Selina would have to milk the cow herself. And if she did not hurry, she told herself wearily, she would have to light a lantern in order to find Clarissa's udder. With a sigh, she turned her steps toward the barn.

Clarissa was still standing where she had left her, tied to the stall, and looking pitiful. Selina swallowed her irritation and smiled.

"You thought I had forgotten you, and it would serve you right if I had. But, as you can see, I have returned."

Now, if the cow would only behave, Selina could finish making the soup before she was too tired to stir it.

She settled herself back down on the stool and held the bucket between her feet. Clarissa, perhaps feeling contrite for running her mistress off, stood perfectly still this time; and, as her milk squirted into the bucket, and her warmth encompassed them both in a sweet-smelling cocoon, Selina's mind began to wander.

It did not have to wander far to light upon Mr. Lint.

His appearance, after they had given him up for lost, would have been welcome at any time, but it had come as a pure blessing today. If they could secure Lord Webb as a customer for their trees by impressing his steward, then other customers should follow. Selina only hoped that Caesar's antics had not ruined their chances of winning him over.

Mr. Lint did not seem to hold the incident against them. Nor had he seemed too discomfited by the notion of conducting his business solely with her. In fact, he had behaved more considerately than she could possibly have wished. Just as he had seemed more the gentleman—and a taller gentleman at that—than she could ever have dreamed.

For a moment, Selina allowed her thoughts to drift back to her first view of him: tall and straight, woolen breeches hugging a pair of strong legs, an elegant jacket fitting his broad shoulders to perfection. Then, when she had stood, she had seen a lean, handsome face, a hint of humor in his blue eyes. And a spark of something else. . . .

There, she chastised herself as she stood to pick up the bucket. She must not go thinking he had admired her looks. He had not gawked, at least. She was used to rude reactions to her height, *and* to ignoring them. Nothing could be done to change her size, and it had come as an advantage under their impoverished circumstances. With no men about, other than Lucas, who was far too old for most chores, it was fortunate she had grown so tall.

All the same, it had been a novel experience to have a man gaze at her so. A man with intelligence, manners, and wit, and not one of the country bumpkins she had grown so used to. Selina sighed. It was almost surprising how elegant he was, but then, a great aristocrat like Lord Webb would naturally have an exceptional man for his steward.

Selina hauled the bucket into the house and covered it, leaving the milk to be skimmed later. That was something Augustus could do. She would miss his help when he was gone. And him.

Not allowing herself to dwell upon that sad day, still in the murky future, she turned to her soup with a will. One beneficial thing about working as hard as she did was the appetite it raised. No matter how exhausted she felt, she could usually summon the energy to make supper. And the stranger's offer to mend the fence had given her enough lift that she hardly felt tired tonight.

By the time Mr. Lint and Augustus had finished setting new rails to the enclosure, Selina had finished the soup and cut and fried great slabs of bacon. Before seeking the laborers out, she retreated upstairs to her room, and ignoring the chill, changed her gown. Her fresh one was as old and out-of-date as the last, but at least it was clean, and she knew its warm colors became her. She brushed the straw out of her hair with a wicked stroke, then tied it back with the yellow ribbons she had bought at the last fair.

She had never had an occasion to wear the ribbons, but Mr. Lint was an important customer and she must do what she could to impress him, she told herself.

With this virtuous thought in mind, Selina walked back downstairs and, needing a lantern now, carried one out to the barn.

The sound of male voices and the clang of metal being scraped helped her to locate the objects of her search. Augustus was cleaning mud from the tools, while laughing at something his companion had said.

The light from Selina's lantern cast a glow upon Mr. Lint, who was unrolling his sleeves in preparation for putting on his jacket. Selina stopped at the doorway, taken aback by the sight of a man's lean chest covered in fine white cotton. Then, seeing streaks of dirt against the white, she was overcome by remorse.

"Oh, dear! I fear your shirt has been ruined."

Mr. Lint glanced down at his chest. His eyes returned to hers, and he smiled. "You mustn't worry. I am sure it can be washed, and if not, I have others."

Of course. He would not be penniless as she and Augustus were.

Selina dismissed this thought, which was unworthy of her, and straightened her shoulders. "My brother and I are very grateful to you for your kind services, Mr. Lint. We would be pleased if you would take your supper with us."

She could see the hesitation in his eyes, and something about it made her lift her chin higher. Undoubtedly he thought he would get a better meal from Mr. Croft.

To her surprise, Mr. Lint accepted her invitation with a graceful bow. Selina thought she had never seen the courtesy performed with such ease. She could imagine that Lord Webb's steward would be at home to an inch in a London ballroom, though, of course, she herself knew nothing of such places.

With his back turned toward her, she watched him put on his coat, a snug-fitting garment that took quite a bit of effort to work into. So much, in fact, that Selina felt her fingers itching to help him into its sleeves. She was amazed that a man who made his living on an estate could afford to waste his time on such an impractical garment, and she began to wonder if Mr. Lint might not have a touch of the dandy in him. His clothes appeared to have been sewn while he stood in them, they fit so well.

Then, as he stretched the jacket over his back, she dismissed such a foolish notion. No man with muscles like his could be a dandy. Selina was used to seeing men's muscles as they worked in the fields: bulging forearms, thick necks, and straining backs. What made this man different was the litheness of his movements, a seemingly unconscious grace that reminded her suddenly, and most uncomfortably, of her father.

Disturbed by this reflection—which was certainly improper, as well as a grim warning that working as she did, she must have developed the sensibilities of a peasant—Selina left Augustus to show Mr. Lint into the house. They joined her as she was cutting the bread.

Mr. Lint paused upon the threshhold. He seemed to take in their situation at a glance—their eating in the kitchen, tallow candles on the table instead of wax, the modesty of their furnishings, even though Selina had set out her mother's old silver.

Fighting the urge to explain that they had not expected company or else she would have opened up the parlor, even going so far as to light a fire in the old chimney place, Selina squared her shoulders.

"If you would care to freshen up, I have warmed some water. It is there by the hearth."

Mr. Lint thanked her, and peeling off his jacket again, set about washing his hands. Augustus shared his soap, then rushed to sit down.

"Augustus. . . ." Selina warned him before he could pinch a slice of bacon. "Do not forget we have a visitor."

Mr. Lint was shrugging himself back into his coat. He tugged at the collar and sleeves as if he were formally dressing for dinner. Selina did not know whether to be amused or gratified by his considerate manners.

He insisted upon waiting for her to be seated, which only complicated the job of serving. In the end, she was obliged to put all the platters and her mother's large soup tureen on the table and to take a chair herself, or he would never have consented to eat.

Flushed by this unaccustomed attention, Selina ladled out the bowls of soup, conscious that the visitor's eyes followed her every movement. "I must apologize," she said to cover the fact that her hand was trembling, "for the behavior of our bull and for the inconvenience he has caused you. Tomorrow, I trust, after you have seen the excellence of our trees, you will not regret having come."

"I do not regret it now."

The sincerity in his voice disturbed her equanimity for a moment, before he continued, "However, I devoutly hope your plan to turn Caesar into a pudding was nothing more than an idle threat."

Selina felt the warmth of embarrassment stealing up to her cheeks at the memory of her outburst. "You must pardon me, sir. I do not mean to give in to my temper, but at times, it will escape."

"Not at all." Mr. Lint accepted the bowl Augustus had passed him. "My concern was purely for the beast. He puts me forcibly in mind of someone I know, though I cannot think just who at the moment. But since that is true, I would hate to see him roasted for drippings."

Augustus laughed, and Selina smiled as her embarrassment faded. "Caesar does have a rather regal air about him. That is why we gave him his name."

"That's it!" Mr. Lint pointed with his spoon before he lowered it to his soup. "I knew he reminded me of someone. He's the Prince Regent to a tee."

Now, even Selina had to put a hand to her lips to keep from laughing. Mr. Lint's eyes met hers over the sputtering candle. They seemed to glow with warmth, and a fluttering rose in her stomach.

"Bread? And bacon?" Selina reached quickly to pass the platters. "Augustus, please serve Mr. Lint some bacon."

In the business of passing the food, she soon conquered her strange feeling, and their three appetites kept them occupied for the moment. Selina was relieved to see that their guest appeared to enjoy what she had cooked.

She knew the fare was simple, but she had learned to cook at her mother's knee, and she was never ashamed of what she served. Of course, she did not often entertain gentlemen, but the vicar had taken an occasional meal with them and had always seemed satisfied. Work, she knew, would give men a taste for food that they might not otherwise have, and Mr. Lint did seem to be appeasing his hunger as he made short work of the slabs of bacon and thick slices of bread.

Perhaps, she thought, relaxing for a moment, he would not regret too much the fare at Mr. Croft's.

A horrible thought made her throat narrow in panic. Mr. Croft would have offered him wine or, at the very least, a tankard of beer. She had no beer in the house.

Rising, she felt a lump of shame deep in the pit of her stomach, as she raised her chin and said, "I have to apologize again, Mr. Lint, but we were not expecting a guest for supper. I cannot offer you ale, but my brother and I are quite partial to cherry wine. Perhaps I could offer you a glass?"

He looked up and blinked once before his excellent manners took over. "I can think of nothing that I would rather have," he said.

Her cheeks warming, for she knew he was simply being polite, Selina went to the cellar cupboard and fetched a fresh bottle of her cherry wine. She took their three remaining glasses to the table—only grateful they still had three—and poured them each one.

"Your good health, Miss—" Mr. Lint seemed to hesitate before he raised his glass to his lips, but then he tasted the wine and complimented her upon it. "Very good. I suppose it was made from your cherries?"

"Yes, I made it myself." Selina could breathe again, now that the embarrassing moment was past. She returned to her chair to find their visitor studying her.

"Forgive me, but"—a frown was on his face—"but surely you do not live alone here? You and your brother?"

"Oh, no." Augustus sprang in, before she could respond. "We have Lucas as well."

"Lucas?"

"Lucas Jones," Selina said rapidly. "He is our servant."

"Oh. I did not see him."

"Lucas is away delivering trees. He makes all our deliveries," Selina said, "as he will for Lord Webb, should you decide to buy our trees."

"Lord Webb?"

His evident confusion puzzled her. "Yes, you did come from Lord Webb, did you not?"

Strangely he seemed to hesitate over his answer. Then, staring at her fixedly, he said, "No, I came upon my own business. I am not acquainted with Lord Webb."

"Oh!" Selina put a hand over her lips. "Oh, you must forgive me. We were expecting Lord Webb's—" She nearly said the word "steward" before she realized that Mr. Lint must not be anyone's servant. And if he were not, how rude it would sound.

She amended it to "—expecting Lord Webb's representative. And when you came today, we quite naturally assumed—"

A fear that he might not be a customer at all suddenly assailed her. "But you have come about trees?"

Again he paused. "Yes. You needn't apologize. I will look forward to seeing them tomorrow. And I quite understand how the confusion of the moment led to this misunderstanding, and, also now why Augustus said you were expecting me."

At this surprising statement, Selina turned to question her brother with a look.

"Mr. Lint gave me a ride home from the village," Augustus explained.

"And in Mr. Croft's gig." Mr. Lint's expression showed that he had just remembered this important fact. "He will be worried that I have made off with it. And I have not yet bespoken a room, so I should be going."

"Oh, dear," Selina said before she could help herself. "And all because of Caesar and my stupidity." She felt crushed with blame as her visitor stood.

"You had nothing to do with it," he said. "I should have had the sense to ask for a room before I left the inn. But the place seemed empty, so I do not doubt there'll be a room for me."

"If there is not," Selina said, following him to the door with a lantern to light his way, "then you must come back here for the night."

Her sense of what was due for his inconvenience had caused her to make the offer, but his reaction surprised her.

Throughout the evening, Mr. Lint had been calm and self-possessed, but now a warm color rose to his face, and a look of something—like chagrin—touched his blue eyes.

"You are very kind, Miss—" Again he paused over her name, and instead of finishing, took her hand and raised it to his lips. "But Mr. Croft is certain to have a room for me. I shall see you both in the morning."

While Selina held the hand he had kissed close to her waist, he turned to Augustus and bid him good night. Then he passed through the door.

Selina thought it only right that she should light his way while he harnessed the horse to the gig, so she followed him to the barn. When he heard her, he looked back and slowed his steps. Unable to think of anything to say, she kept silent while, side by side, they covered the short distance from the house.

Mr. Lint worked quickly and quietly, and soon he was leading the horse outside. Eager to get home, Mr. Croft's horse backed willingly into her traces. Selina held the lantern high, while Mr. Lint attached the various pieces of harness. When he was done, he thanked her for her help.

"You should be getting to your bed," he told her, "or Clarissa will have to wake you herself."

"Oh." Selina laughed. "Augustus will milk her. That is his chore, not mine." Something in his tone had started a melting feeling, like wine deep inside her stomach.

"In that case," he said before leaving, "if I were you, I should have him turn Caesar out again."

"Oh? And why is that?"

He took her hand, and his lips brushed her fingertips once more. "If I am not mistaken"—he released her to climb up into the gig—"and mind you, I am only judging by the gleam I saw in Caesar's eye, I think he does mean to have his way with Clarissa sooner than you think."

Before she could react with a startled "Oh!" and a touch to her lips, he had flicked the horse with the reins and started forward.

Selina wanted to bite her tongue right out of her mouth. She had to remember to keep her mouth shut, to remember all those things her mother had taught her, and not to give up on being a lady no matter how low they had sunk.

But to think that Mr. Lint had heard her say such an indelicate thing!

She hurried back into the house, wondering how she would face him on the morrow.

She would have been comforted, perhaps, to know that Richard was cursing himself at that moment for giving in to the urge to dally with her. How could he have been so unprincipled?

To flirt with a girl—an unprotected girl, no matter what they said about this Lucas fellow—and especially a girl he had come to harass was an impardonable offense. He could only plead the light from a full moon as his defense. It had shone down so upon her hair and those simple yellow ribbons. He did not think he had ever seen anything so lovely as those inexpensive bits of golden satin against the brown silk of her hair.

He could not deny that he found her attractive. She was what one might have called in an older and far less delicate age "a strapping wench." But a wench with the carriage and curves of a goddess. That proud little lift of her chin, her air of command, and her gracious manners when she wasn't cursing at her bull—and even her cursing he had found appealing—all combined to make her very attractive indeed. There was no question that he found her desirable, but that was no excuse for his self-indulgence.

He had come to read her brother a lecture upon the dignity of his ancient family. Then, finding Augustus blameless, he had searched for a different object for his ire. After spending the entire evening at the Grange, he was no closer to knowing who had trespassed upon his name than he had been before. He only knew that Selina had used it shamelessly and freely. The anger he had felt when he had read the Garter's letter had long since dissipated, and now he found himself more curious than mad.

Although ... The more Richard reflected upon the evening, the more certain he was that there had been a touch of defensiveness in Selina's manner when she had introduced herself. Perhaps Miss Payley was not so innocent as she seemed.

Tomorrow he would have to confront her. The confusion this evening had served to put him off. That, and the distress Selina had shown over Caesar's eating her trees.

Richard could not have brought himself to add to her distress at that moment, not when he had detected the fragility beneath her intrepid demeanor.

It had taken no more than one look at that kitchen and the modesty of their meal for him to realize what kind of life they led. He ought not to have accepted her invitation to sup, but something had told him her pride would be wounded if he did not. He had meant to tell her the truth at the table, and the perfect opportunity had offered itself. But, again, for her distress—

When she had discovered he was not the customer she had expected, her alarm had deflected him from his purpose again. He knew it was due to a financial disappointment. His natural reaction had been to promise to look at her trees, and presumably to buy some. He would make good on that promise. Tomorrow, however, and without fail, he would discover why she was using his name and upon whose authority. He would tell her who he was and why he had come before the situation became even more tangled.

Having made this decision, Richard arrived at Mr. Croft's inn and was so fortunate as to find a room for the night. The innkeeper's relief upon having his gig returned to him amused Richard, for he was not often suspected of being a thief.

When Mr. Croft asked his name, however, he hesitated, then gave the name Lint. If he divulged his title, and the news preceded him to the Grange the next morning, he had no doubt he would be treated to quite a different reception from the one he had been given today. Besides, it was not at all unusual for aristocrats to travel incognito, and Mr. Croft would be likely to become anxious, and more than a little curious as to Richard's mission, if he knew he was entertaining the Earl of Linton.

The room Richard was shown was more modest than any he had ever had the privilege to sleep in, but it was clean and the sheets were well aired. Mrs. Croft, who acted as chambermaid, seemed a tidy person, so he did not fear the possibility of lice.

After an hour of hard labor, to which he was not in the least accustomed, Richard felt more than ready to retire. When he looked at his timepiece, he laughed to realize that the hour was no more advanced than eight o'clock. The short winter day and country hours had conspired to make him think it quite late, when if he were in London, he would just then be leaving his house for the evening's enjoyment.

The remarkable thing was how good it felt to be physically tired, as if he had just completed an all-day hunt. He would sleep well tonight. If he had wished for a change from his London rounds, he had certainly found it here in Uckfield.

The only things he had missed were his valet's attentions and his evening drink. His valet could not be conjured up, but the drink surely could. Richard asked Mr. Croft to draw him a pint of his best beer, which he savored with his feet propped before the fire as he shuddered at the thought of that cherry wine.

Good God! but he had never tasted anything so foul. Good manners had forced him to drink it, but he had been taken aback—much more than aback—by Selina's offer of it.

Again, the thought of wounding her pride had governed him. He knew the signs by then: her nose held high in the air, her shoulders straightened, and an unconscious toss of her hair. As he set his tankard down, that memory made him smile. He hoped to be spared any more of her wine. As far as he was concerned, the only good thing about it had been the way it had colored Selina's lips a deep red. They had looked as plump and ripe and luscious as the cherry itself.

With the thought of those tempting lips, and Selina's ripeness, Richard dozed off in his chair, Mr. Croft's excellent porter forgotten at his side.

Chapter Four

$\mathcal{L}$ong before Richard had finished dressing for breakfast, Selina was up and working. While Augustus milked the cow, she fed the chickens and collected the eggs. Then, after making breakfast for the two of them, she hurriedly tidied up their dishes before going into the garden to pull up turnips and greens for the hog.

Once these were boiled and cooled, she mixed them in a bucket with a share of Clarissa's milk, and the leavings from breakfast and last night's supper. Wrapped up against the cold, she made her way to the pig's pen, hoping to finish this most undignified of her chores before Mr. Lint could catch her at it. She would have asked Augustus to feed the pig, but because of last night's debacle, he had not been able to clean out the stalls, and that absolutely had to be done before Clarissa risked hoof rot.

All the same, today of all days, Selina wished she did not have to feed the hog. Say what one would about the charm of pigs, their undoubted intelligence, and the undeniable appeal of piglets, Selina did not think any gentleman would see treating the hog to a bucket of slops as a proper chore for a lady. Keeping company with swine did not show one to best advantage.

Not—Selina reminded herself as she rounded the barn—not that she had any foolish designs upon Mr. Lint. Why, she hardly knew him. It was simply not that

43

often that a strange gentleman—especially one with such urbane manners—was expected to call. Such a thing, in fact, had never happened in all her nineteen years. Mr. Lint's appearance had something of a mystery about it. Now that she thought it over, he never had mentioned precisely what his business was. Or why he had come. Or from where.

But—Selina dismissed these facts as the result of last night's circumstances. They had been too busy, all of them, to engage in idle chatter. It had taken her halfway through dinner just to discover that he was not who she thought he was.

And then he had left so suddenly. She might not have believed he had come if it were not for the mended fence and the memory of her blushes.

Anxiously switching her bucket from one hand to the next, Selina worried that something in her manner might have led Mr. Lint to flirt with her. Something unladylike, perhaps, such as her swearing. Or worse—she faltered in her stride—that invitation to sleep at the Grange, which had made him so uncomfortable. Convinced that was it, she determined today to give him no such cause to think her vulnerable to his charm. Nothing would be more fatal to her true design, which was selling him cartloads of trees, than to appear to be weak. That would indicate she was a poor man of business.

Woman, that was.

She could never let it be said that she had seduced a potential customer, nor could she open herself to a rumor that she had been seduced. Augustus, and this place, were depending upon her, and unmarried women in her position might be seen as fair game. She had to watch her every step.

And ... even more important to Selina, she would not have Mr. Lint thinking her so desperate that she

44

would fling herself at the first available gentleman to stroll by.

With this resolve firmly tacked in place, she arrived at the pen to find that Nero was in trouble. A vast black hog of some fifty stone, he had backed himself into a corner, dislodged a rotten board from the fence, and stuck his hoof right through it. He did not seem to have noticed that the board was still affixed to his leg, since he was rooting quite peacefully. Then, in his clever way, he greeted her with a grunt. He started forward much too fast in anticipation of his breakfast—

With a clunk, the board, which he had dragged along, struck the corner of his water trough. Nero stumbled with a squeal. The board dug into his leg. It must have pained him for he began to back, then go forward, then back, then forward, faster and faster, all the while squealing as if he were being roasted on a spit.

The noise was so strident, Selina wanted nothing more than to run and cover her ears, but she could not let his leg be broken. She dropped her bucket, then swooped up her skirts, and tried to reach inside the pen for the board.

"Oh, you stupid"—as he turned his snout toward her to defend himself from her ministrations, she minded her language—"you stupid *swine*! Why do I bother with you? You have been nothing but a trial!"

The squeals brought Augustus running. "What's he done this time?" At a glance the boy saw what was wrong and leapt into the pen.

His presence, and the threat now of two people bearing down upon him, only added to Nero's panic. He ran madly about the pen, splattering Selina's face and dress with cold mud.

She could hardly keep herself from cursing. "I'll turn you into bacon, you—you—I'll—"

"—string him up and make a ham out of him?" an amused voice cut calmly through the din.

In sudden anguish Selina whirled to see Mr. Lint rolling up his sleeves behind her. He had already removed his tight-fitting coat to reveal another spotless white shirt.

"No, you must not!" she warned him, waving him off. "You must not get soiled again on our account."

"Nonsense," he answered coolly, stepping into the fray. "Do you think I would just watch while you brave this angry glutton? More importantly, should I stand by while a poor afflicted beast is treated to threat upon threat? What is his name, by the way?" He asked this casually, as he picked up a stout stick to back the pig into a corner.

"Nero," Selina supplied, laughing helplessly at his sally, though she felt as close to tears.

"Then, Nero, I must warn you that Miss Selina will have you tied and packed in brine before you can count to three if you do not cooperate. Be ready to grab the board," Mr. Lint said this to Augustus, rather in the manner of a knight commanding his squire.

Selina had already seen in what direction he was headed, and had taken a place on the outside near the corner post. With herself on one side and Augustus on the other, they just might manage to catch the board.

Mr. Lint was skillfully backing Nero, his stick poised like a sword to halt the hog's flanking attempts.

Just before Nero's rump reached the corner, he gave the word, "Grab the board . . . now!"

Both Selina and her brother grasped it and managed to hold on while the pig, startled by their movement, lunged forward. They pulled backward, straining against the hog's immense strength, until his leg was extended behind him. In another second the rotten board slipped free, and they both fell back into the dirt.

Squealing in terror, Nero charged forward. Selina was ready to scream, but Mr. Lint dodged him, stepping aside as if to avoid a rapier thrust. He turned to anticipate another charge, but the silly pig had just that quickly realized that he'd been freed and had calmed instantly. Like the single-minded beast he was, he rooted up to the fence and stood, oinking for his meal.

Mr. Lint let out a laugh, tossed his stick across the fence, and vaulted lightly to the other side. Turning, he saw that Selina was struggling to her feet and hastened to help.

Dirt had coated her palms when she had tried to catch herself. Muck—that evil pig's muck—had soiled her dress. And Mr. Lint had no more grace than to look, with the exception of his mud-caked boots, as spotless as a baby in a christening gown.

"Are you quite all right?" he asked her, ignoring the dust on her hand as he took it to pull her up.

Selina did her best to snatch it back. "Yes, I am. Thank you very much. But you must not—"

Her protests, however, were useless. Nothing she could say would dissuade Mr. Lint from dusting off the back of her gown even though half the dirt he raised landed on his breeches. Not even her embarrassment, which she thought must be quite in evidence, seemed to discourage him.

And, as if that were not enough, he extracted a handkerchief—a fine white linen handkerchief—from the pocket of his breeches to wipe her face.

"If you'll permit," he said, then proceeded to ignore her protests, "you've a smudge on your face."

"A smudge! Sir, your manners are so perfect as to astound me! Why, I must have half a mud puddle on my face! Which you should not, as I've tried to tell you, use your handkerchief to erase. I can very well take care of it myself. Inside. As is proper. If you will just be so kind as to stop daubing at me." Selina hoped she did not sound too upset, but truly this had been the outside of enough!

Mr. Lint took no offense. He lowered his handkerchief with a grin and bowed. "Certainly, miss, you may proceed as you think fit. I only hoped to assist, much as Sir Walter Raleigh must have done with Queen Elizabeth. You'll remember the legend of his cloak? Unfortunately I have not brought my cloak with me, or it would lie at your feet."

At such nonsense Selina could do nothing but laugh. Her laughter was mixed with mortification, but it helped that Mr. Lint found something to amuse him in the episode. It surprised her that a man who made his living on the land could find anything having to do with farm animals amusing—not when they were repeatedly getting into trouble—which made her wonder again exactly what his position was.

Before she could wonder too long, however, he changed the subject. "Why Nero?" he asked. "Is he mad?"

"As near as makes no difference," Augustus chimed in. He had dusted himself off and came to join them with a toss of his fine hair. "He's always getting into mad starts."

"The last of which I have just been privileged to witness. Come along, Squire," Mr. Lint said, ruffling Augustus's hair. "Let's fix that pen while your sister's composing herself."

Before they did, however, he grabbed the bucket and treated Nero to what he'd been grunting for.

Composing herself was right, Selina decided as she picked her way to the house, lifting her skirts with as much dignity as she could muster. She had worried about Mr. Lint finding her feeding the pig, and he had caught her wrestling with it instead. How demure! How refined!

Fuming all the way to the house, she reminded herself that it did not matter what he thought as long as he bought her trees. He was, after all, no more than a customer to her. She should be glad to have entertained him when he might have gone off in disgust.

Although he didn't seem to be in such a great hurry to leave, she noted. Selina put aside all thought of asking where he came from. She could not risk offending him with an interrogation. He had shown such patience, how could she treat him to suspicion? It did not matter anyway, in the long run, just where he had sprung from. And in the short run, his help had been quite useful. She made no doubt that he would be gone from the district by morning, but she would not be in a hurry to chase him off.

Richard watched her go with an appreciative quirk to his lips. Even with pig-muck splattered all over her, Selina had managed to look regal. It *had* amused him greatly to find himself chasing a hog around its pen. What his friends or the society matrons would say if they had seen him, he did not know. He only knew he had not had so much fun since he was a boy.

But he had not meant to wound Selina's pride. Her pride was clearly what kept her going in the face of so much adversity. In her circumstances it was a marvelous trait. He wondered, however, how that pride would transfer into other, less arduous spheres. An assembly of ladies and gentlemen, for instance. Would she look down her nose at all their pretensions . . . like a countess?

His own quest for a countess sprang into his mind, jolting him out of his reverie. An image of Selina putting Wilfrid in his place had been surprisingly pleasing.

. . . Disturbingly so.

Richard remembered his reason for coming to Uckfield,

which had slipped his mind the moment he had seen Selina struggling with the pig. Now would certainly not be a good time to straighten out her misapprehension. He made no doubt that her pride had been wounded enough by being discovered in such an undignified act. And, even though he himself had found nothing remotely unattractive in her doings—to the contrary, he had only admired her courage and spunk—he knew that ladies could be a bit prickly when issues of vanity were involved.

No, the time was definitely not right. Perhaps later when she had shown him her trees and he had conducted his purchase, he would find a more appropriate opportunity to confess his lie.

But, he thought with a smile, if Selina did not keep from running into trouble, there might never be an appropriate moment.

When Selina returned in less than half an hour, he and Augustus had finished their work on the pen. She arrived wearing a different gown. It, too, was faded and out-of-date. Like the last, however, this skirt fell in ample folds from her waist and seemed to suit her noble stature. Richard admired the way it swayed with every one of her steps.

He also noted with pleasure the fresh gleam of her face, the result of a hard scrubbing with soap. And the shine of her hair, which could only have been achieved by a vigorous brushing owed to her magnificent rage. He would not have been at all surprised to learn that the boar bristles—as a surrogate for Nero—had been subjected to a hundred strokes, the gloss on her locks was so high.

Out of tact, however, he affected not to notice any change when Selina thanked him with her noble air and invited him to accompany her to the orchard. With a bow he followed her, not missing the fact that for all her apparent confidence, she would not meet his eye.

And seemed determined not to do so. As they walked toward the orchard, Richard found that he had to race to match her stride. With her womanly proportions her legs were nearly as long as his, which allowed her to stay a shoulder's depth in front of him. Plainly she was used to working at top speed. Richard wondered if she ever had a second to rest from her chores.

He followed her into the orchard and through the rows of mature trees as she pointed out the strength of her stock. Never stopping for more than a second or two beside any one, she kept him hastening to keep up. Unfamiliar with the terrain, he barely had time to see what she was pointing out and to watch his step as they charged from row to row and tree to tree.

Richard hoped he was making suitable noises of interest in response to her descriptions, but he could not see her face well enough to tell. All he saw was the curve of her high cheekbone, the softer line of her jaw, and occasionally a glimpse of her lush, full lips. He wished he could forget the sight of those lips, their color deepened by cherry wine. Such a memory was not very conducive to recalling his business.

Arriving at the end of a row, Selina did not pause, but turned and retraced her steps to the fence, double-paced. With an inward grin Richard let her lead. Miss Selina Whoever-She-Was did not appear to get over an indignity very easily.

She led him into the seedling orchard, where Caesar had done his damage. A damage that was distressingly evident in the morning light.

Selina, however, seemed to pay the destruction no mind as she strode past the nibbled trees to reach the ones that had been spared.

"These are the seedlings from which you might select, Mr. Lint." Her tone begged him to do just that.

Richard was not yet ready to have their business concluded, for he still had not discovered what he had come to find out. And he could see that she was not ready to learn that the customer she needed so badly was, in reality, a peer with a grudge.

He stalled a bit longer.

"We passed a number of young trees before arriving at these," he said, anticipating her answer.

What he had not foreseen was her reaction. The mention of the ruined trees had the impact of a blow to her face.

"Yes," she managed to get out, "but those have quite likely been damaged beyond salvation. I would not try to sell you those."

"That is not what I meant," he hastened to assure her. "I was simply wondering what you would do with them now."

Selina gave a half shrug, a brave gesture. "Oh, we shall have to look them over individually. See if there is anything to be spared."

"Who will prune them?"

"Myself . . . Augustus . . ." As an afterthought, she added, "Lucas."

Richard knew he must have frowned, for her chin rose in the air. "You need not concern yourself, Mr. Lint. We have had such setbacks before. As you yourself know, such are the risks of farming."

Richard did know. But his setbacks had never cost him in relative terms what this episode would cost Selina. That knowledge pained him inexplicably and made him reluctant to let the subject drop.

He changed it instead to something related. "Your man, Lucas—you say he is due to return soon?"

Again he seemed to have caught her unprepared. A shadow touched her face.

"Yes. He should have been back by now, but I expect he will be shortly."

"Is he a trustworthy sort of fellow? What I mean is can he be trusted to do as he's bid?"

Her answer was evasive. So were her eyes as they sought a spot on the ground. "Whether he can be or not is not the issue, for I must have a man to perform such tasks." She flushed, and her eyes met his for one brief glance. "You yourself were surprised, I make no doubt, to discover an unmarried lady running her family's estate. And, although you made no protest, there are others who are not so charitable as to condescend to do business with me. Lucas allows me to conduct our affairs under the cloak of my brother's name without most people being the wiser."

"And has it served?"

"It serves reasonably well," she said, turning away.

Richard kept apace with her as she pointed out certain seedlings he might think it wise to choose, but all he could think of was the rot on every fence, the sagging roof to the house, and the fields that should have been turned by this time of year and had not. If this Lucas was their servant, why had he not performed this job, when to all appearances, Selina and her brother did all the work in the house and barn? And now, this Lucas-person was returning late.

Just as Richard had this last thought, the sound of cart wheels came up the drive. He turned with Selina.

"Lucas!" The relief in her voice was palpable, though she tried to hide it. In an aside marked by an assumed confidence, she said, "You see, Mr. Lint, I told you he would be back at any moment. If you will excuse me, however, I should go see just how he fared."

Richard agreed with a bow of the head, but instead of staying where he was, followed her out of the orchard. He wanted to see for himself just who this Lucas was.

The object of his gaze was rather slovenly in appearance. Lucas's hair, turning gray, must have been left as it had been slept upon, for no cap could have produced such disarray. His face was grizzled with a few days of whiskers growing unevenly on his upper lip and jaw. Slow to get down from his cart, he shuffled none too sprightly across the yard.

Selina asked him whether his business had been completed, then repeated the question when he seemed reluctant to hand over his purse. Lucas's eyes followed the money longingly, as if he had hoped against hope that she would forget to ask for it. Selina opened the purse right away, appeared to make a quick count, then handed Lucas back some coins, which he quickly retrieved and stuffed into the pocket of his vest.

Despite some signs of aging, Richard perceived that much of the man's slowness was nothing more than an act. His deafness was certainly assumed, for it turned remarkably around the moment Selina inquired whether he had breakfasted.

"Not so's you'd notice," he mumbled pitifully, doffing his cap and wiping his nose upon his sleeve.

"Then, you will want to help yourself to the bacon I've saved for you. It's wrapped by the fire, along with a piece of bread."

"Thank 'ee, Mistress Payley."

His use of her name recalled Richard's business to him just as the older man turned in search of his food. His step was far more lively until he remembered to shuffle.

"Something of a character," Richard said after him, hoping to draw Selina out.

She only smiled, a smile of distinct intelligence. "He

is. Lucas would have me think he is much too decrepit for farmwork, but I've noticed how well he accomplishes the things he wishes to do. On his nights off, he has no trouble harnessing the horse to the cart to go to Mr. Croft's."

She said this with a deep chuckle, and Richard wished he could laugh along with her, but he was much too annoyed by the reality. A girl and her brother, who was no more than a boy, managing this place with no able-bodied man about? To all appearances, Lucas was next to useless. *For* appearances, he might serve some simple purpose, but surely for nothing else.

Without more help the Grange and the two who occupied it were doomed to a slow and painful ruin.

Richard had scarcely come to this distressing conclusion when the sound of another arrival caught his ear. Selina, too, had heard the horse's hooves. She raised her head, and before she could hide it, a flash of comical pain crossed her features.

Richard looked to see who had earned her disgust, and was surprised to find a young Adonis approaching on a steed of the drafting variety. The picture they made was quite impressive: a young man, strong as an ox by the look of him and handsome in a florid sort of way, perched upon a horse that could easily have carried two knights in full armor.

Turning back to see if he had been mistaken in his interpretation of Selina's welcome, he found the annoyed look gone. In its place was a patient smile.

"Good day t' you, Mistress Payley." The youth tipped his hat, which, though not of the first elegance, showed the possession of some fortune. He had the air of a wealthy farmer, not that of a gentleman. "Got a visitor, have you?"

Noting the name the man had used to address her—

Payley again, and not Trevelyan—Richard made his bow while Selina performed her introductions.

Mr. Fancible, it appeared, was heir to the neighboring farm, which explained Selina's casual way of greeting him. It was clear that the two had been acquainted since childhood, for Selina did not stand on any ceremony, but told him in no uncertain terms that she was occupied.

This did not stop Mr. Fancible from dismounting from his horse. And, when he did, Richard experienced something that struck him in a most unpleasant way. At over six feet, he had always been taller than most of his acquaintance. He had become accustomed to the gentle feeling of superiority his height afforded him.

But this young man loomed over him. So much so that Richard would have considered Mr. Fancible grossly misshapen, had his proportions not been so perfect.

As it was, Richard could only stand in awe of the pair of shoulders that dwarfed his own not inconsiderable pair. Mr. Fancible's wrists, which showed at the bottom of his cuffs, could each make two of most of the men's in London. Richard wondered just what the young man's mother had eaten to produce such a healthy specimen, one who reeked so strongly of masculinity as to make his own hackles rise.

"Won't be no bother," Mr. Fancible said, ignoring Selina's broad hint. "Just come to see how that pig of yours is getting on."

"Nero is perfectly fine," Selina told him, forgetting somehow to mention the adventure of the morning. "You needn't worry about him so."

A touch of exasperation tinged her voice. Richard wondered whether this was a ruse Mr. Fancible had used before to give himself a reason for coming by. If so, it was a very feeble one.

"Has Nero been ill?" Richard inquired politely. "Is that the reason for your call?"

"Eh?" Mr. Fancible turned toward him. Richard could see that the conversation had moved much too swiftly for his stunted brain.

Selina answered in his stead, while a flush she could not hide struggled up her neck. "No, he has not been ill, but Mr. Fancible was kind enough to sell Nero to me. And he has been worried about the condition of that pen."

Richard had no sooner nodded to indicate his understanding than Mr. Fancible said with the air of someone who had repeated himself a hundred times. "Time for you to let me fix that fence."

Selina crossed her arms. "I told you that Lucas would soon get to it, and in fact, the fence has been repaired just this morning. So you can see that there is no reason for you to be so concerned." Her tone when giving this speech was so firm, only a simpleton could ignore it.

Richard did not miss the fact that she had made it sound as if Lucas, not he, had done the job. Did she fear the young man's jealousy?

In any event her tone had no effect upon Mr. Fancible's sensibilities, for he ignored it entirely. "Fixed it, did he? Well, let's have a look."

With a swinging movement, much like an elephant on the march, Mr. Fancible turned and lumbered slowly toward the barn.

Selina had had enough. Starting after him, her fists clenched tightly at her sides, she called out, "Romeo! I will not be accompanying you. Mr. Lint and I are conducting business."

Romeo? On hearing the name, Richard suppressed a grin. The lad had certainly been well tagged. Many a Juliet would swoon over a man of his size and figure, not to mention his dark, curly hair and his well-featured countenance.

Richard looked for signs of swooning in Selina and was rewarded by seeing none. He had hoped she would have better taste than to fall for this bumpkin. For it should not take anyone long to see that Romeo's virtues, though perhaps more than skin deep, certainly did not reach as far as his brain.

The truth was, handsome or no, the man was an oaf and a boor.

Selina turned back at that moment and must have noticed the amusement lurking in Richard's eyes, for she raised her chin in the air.

"Mr. Fancible has known us all our lives and takes a kindly interest in our affairs. It is not at all unlike him to offer his services."

"Services you had rather not accept?" Richard asked, falling into step beside her as she marched back toward the trees. "I can see why you would rather not be obliged to such a clod. Would you like me to send him about his business?"

He had spoken without thinking.

He soon discovered his remarks had crossed the bounds when Selina whirled on him, her eyes flashing with indignation. "No, thank you, Mr. Lint. For you see, I shall quite likely marry that clod one day!"

Chapter Five

"Marry? Him?" The shock of incredulity hit Richard in the chest. The strength of his reaction shamed and amazed him, even as he spoke.

He could see that he had startled Selina as well. She recoiled, her eyes opened wide, and she seemed to skip a breath.

"Yes," she said, recovering enough to toss her head. "And, pray, why does that notion astound you?"

"Because—my dear girl, you have more breeding in your little finger than that farmer has in his entire body."

She flushed. Her lips gave a rueful twist. He was not sure whether his compliment had pleased or dismayed her.

But he was wrong to be saying such things to a lady he hardly knew. Wrong to be taking a position on a personal matter that did not regard him at all.

"You must pardon me," he offered with an awkward bow, "if my ill-considered remarks have offended you. They were not made with any intention to wound—with any intention at all, in fact. I was simply surprised. . . ." He let his words trail away, feeling inadequate to explain his violent reaction, though the notion of such a *mésalliance* still rankled.

An oaf like that, making off with such a magnificent creature? The thought was inconceivable.

Selina accepted his apology with a slight nod and continued their walk back to the orchard. From time to time along the way, she cast him a sideways glance.

Feeling distinctly uncomfortable—almost *de trop*—Richard thought the time had finally come to disclose his true business at the Grange before his strange interest in the Payleys could become any deeper. It would be the height of absurdity for him to embroil himself in their affairs.

He could not deny his desire to do so. It was growing stronger with every bit of evidence that showed him how poorly suited they were to fend for themselves. A stunning girl, who ought by all rights to be gracing the finest drawing rooms, consorting with pigs and suchlike? With no more help than a boy? Why, the whole situation was preposterous!

Richard convinced himself it was the gross injustice of it all that had captured his concern when he knew he had no right to give in to these feelings. What could he give the Payleys, after all, except a few instances of meager assistance? He could offer them charity, but he doubted very much that Selina would accept it.

Before he could grapple with this question, Selina spoke in a hesitant voice. "You must not berate yourself for speaking so plainly. I had no right to speak of Mr. Fancible as I did—"

"Not at all—"

"It is just that we have known each other from birth. And although my father would have disapproved the match—thinking the connection"—she stumbled—"not quite eligible for his family, perhaps—I cannot afford to be so nice."

She kept her gaze straight in front of her, her arms crossed as she walked. Though she took a deep breath, she did not slow her pace. "The truth is, Mr. Lint, that I will not be able to farm this place alone, once Augustus is gone."

From the stiffness in her carriage, Richard could tell how much the admission had cost her, as well as the degree to which such a prospect distressed her.

He muttered his acknowledgment, all the while protesting vehemently inside. Unable to contain his impatience entirely, he finally said, "I meant no disparagement of Mr. Fancible. I am sure he is a respectable man of many virtues. It was—forgive me—simply the disparity in class that caught me off guard. Are there no more eligible gentlemen in the vicinity?"

He should have foreseen her answer, and to do her credit, it was uttered with a laugh. "If there are, sir, they do not spend their time in farmyards. Nor have I had occasion to move about in the first circles. Our means are much too constricted for that."

"But surely—I mean, there must be fellows about the county. Gentlemen who take an interest in their estates, as I do?"

Selina's lips quivered with amusement. "And who do not mind being towered over by a lady? You do them much too much credit, sir."

Richard's stomach clenched at her implied criticism of her own attractions, no matter how lightly said. He hoped Selina had some inkling of how plentiful they were. Richard recalled his feelings the first time he had seen her—as if he'd been kicked in the chest.

"Any man with two eyes in his head would only have to glance at you once to be besotted," he said much more fervently than he'd intended.

A sudden indrawn breath seemed to render her speechless. A smile trembled at the corners of her mouth, a dimple peeked from one rounded cheek, before she suppressed them both and turned aside.

Richard found himself looking with pleasure on the warm tones of her skin and the modest fall of her lashes. He was used to beautiful women. London was full of them—though not in Selina's hearty style. It must be the natural quality of her beauty that he found so appealing, he decided.

But his gaze must have lingered too long for his own good. Something stirred in his loins, and he had to cough while he forcibly turned his thoughts to cherry trees.

The clop of a horse's hooves saved him from a moment rife with dangers. Mr. Fancible caught up with them on the back of his steed.

He tipped his hat again to Richard, then leaned down to speak to Selina. "That's a poor job Lucas did. Pig'll have that board down again in a wink."

Though unintentional, his criticism caused Richard to bristle.

Good Lord! he muttered to himself. Just let this Romeo fellow try mending a pen with no good boards around!

Selina had squirmed guiltily at Romeo's inadvertent insult. Now she glanced at Richard's face and seemed to find something in his expression to amuse her.

"I daresay Lucas was not *himself* when he undertook the job," she said to Romeo with only a slight emphasis for Richard's sake. "He's been telling me for some time that he's not up to such strenuous work."

Richard's good humor returned in the face of her teasing, but Romeo's next words erased it again.

"Better let me see to such things."

Selina stiffened.

Her reaction, however, was not nearly so great as Richard's, who felt his spine go rigid. This Romeo certainly knew how to get under a fellow's skin.

Richard itched to give him a set-down, but Selina was handling the situation in her own practiced way. "You are kind, Romeo, but we can manage quite well on our own, thank you." She cut a sideways glance Richard's way, then said, quite unnecessarily he thought, "But we shall be sure to call upon you whenever our troubles warrant your help."

Romeo seemed to be satisfied, although it was clear he was not ready to be dismissed. His gaze lingered on Selina's face—shyly and respectfully—long after she thanked him for riding over and bade him good day. After a firm repetition of her good-bye, he finally pointed his horse's nose in the opposite direction and plodded off.

Richard felt a strange tension in his shoulders, as if he had readied for a challenge. Which was ludicrous, he thought. Breathing deeply, he eased the muscles in his neck.

Augustus, whom neither one had seen since Nero's temper tantrum, came running up the drive. In his hand he waved a folded sheet of paper.

If Richard had realized the boy had planned to go into the village, he would have lent him his horse. He was on the point of saying so when Augustus called out, "It's from the Garter King of Arms!"

His news smacked Richard soundly in the face. He had been sure the Garter would have notified the Payleys of his refusal of their claim long before his arrival. Otherwise, he would never have allowed himself to be caught in such an awkward position. He was the last person who should be present when Selina read the Garter's letter.

But there was nothing he could do to avoid it. Selina sprang for the missive and tore the seal before Richard could excuse himself.

The change in her expression—from a boundless hope, which had made her eyes sparkle, to a bottomless despair, which made her suddenly go pale—nearly tore his heart. In no little measure, he felt to blame for her sadness, even though his own responsibility was nil. He wished he did not so keenly identify now with her well-being. Or with Augustus's, for the boy seemed to take the letter's contents as hard as his sister did.

"Distressing news?" Richard could not prevent himself from begging the opportunity to console.

"Yes ... I'm afraid so." Selina's eyes met his. A thought, like a brief plea for sympathy, seemed to move behind them as she said, "We've been denied the use of our ancestor's coat of arms."

"On what grounds?" Richard asked, feeling the veriest weasel for pretending, but at last, on the verge of discovering what he had come to find out. And it was possible that he could do so now without divulging his real identity.

The more he thought about it, the more he was coming to believe things would be better left that way. He had far rather part from these people a stranger in harmony than let his duplicity add to their misery. He meant them no harm. In fact, he was prepared to buy tens—hundreds—a thousand trees if it would help them.

Selina's chin was already on the way up when she answered, "On the grounds that our proof of kinship is not substantial enough."

"And is it?"

He had pushed for too much. Selina was obviously beginning to regret her openness.

"Of course," she said with a toss of her proud head. "I am quite certain of where I stand." But her eyes avoided his as she said in a lower voice, "If you will excuse me, I think I should prepare something for dinner—that is, if you would be willing to postpone our business until later?"

Richard hurriedly assured her that he would be willing

to wait, knowing she meant to hide her distress, though he wondered how much longer he should stay at the Grange. His feelings for the Payleys were growing far too complex. The quick embrace that Selina gave her brother in passing revealed too much for Richard's heart to take lightly. The bond of love between them. Their joint disappointment. Though it did not reveal the reason for their dismay.

Intending to be of help to one of them, since he could not be to the other, Richard offered the boy his assistance in pruning the trees. Augustus accepted it with good grace, showing once again how well he had been raised. The proof of breeding, Richard knew, was not in one's family tree so much as in the gentility one displayed. And these Payleys had gentility in abundance—frustrated gentility, trodden down—but gentility nonetheless.

He begged Augustus to tutor him in the way of pruning cherry trees, giving his future plans of an immense planting as reason. The two fetched tools from a drafty outbuilding, which could have stood a new roof, then set to their task. They worked side by side for many minutes, Augustus showing him just where to clip each trunk in the hope of saving the seedlings. The boy's manner of instruction was polite. Far too polite, as Richard found when Augustus's use of his false name flailed him again and again, reminding him of his own high-handed arrogance, his unwarranted temper on receiving the Garter's letter, and his continuing duplicity.

"Listen here, young Squire," Richard finally said in exasperation. "It seems to me that two gentlemen working side by side as equals should address each other with a little less formality. Why do you not call me Richard instead."

"As you wish." Augustus grinned and tossed the hair back out of his eyes. Being referred to as a gentleman and treated as such had obviously pleased him. "But if Selina rakes me over the coals for being too familiar, I hope you will be around to protest."

"You have my word." Richard paused, then added casually, "The same should go for her, however. If we three were not partners this morning when chasing down your pig, I do not know what we were."

"Perhaps more a matador with his banderilleros?"

At the learned response Richard lifted his head in surprise. "Where did you hear of such things as bullfights?"

"I've been reading a good deal." Augustus shrugged, but Richard could see he was grossly understating the case. "I'm being tutored, you know, by the vicar."

"No, I did not know," Richard replied. "To what end?"

To his dismay, chagrin swept Augustus's face.

Thinking that his question might have implied a lack of faith in the boy's abilities, Richard amended it hastily. "I am sure your ambitions are well-deserved. I only inquire as to their nature."

The boy's eyes did not clear. A troubled frown settled on his face as he bent over a nibbled tree with his pair of lopping shears.

"I was hoping to go to Eton," he said, "but I doubt I shall now."

"And why is that?"

The boy shrugged as if there were something he did not mean to divulge. Or perhaps he simply did not wish to confess that they lacked the money to pay for a boy's stay at Eton.

Unless . . . Richard thought he might have tumbled to the truth . . . unless they found a patron. A wealthy kinsman perhaps. A Trevelyan.

Was that the reason they had applied for his name? So Selina might approach him on Augustus's behalf?

Seeking to discover their secret, sure it had something

to do with their claim to his name, Richard asked, "Have you a sponsor?"

Augustus shook his head. "I *had* been meaning to go as a King's Scholar."

"A—" Richard caught himself before he could blurt out his shock. *A King's Scholar*, for Christ's sake! His stomach revolted at the thought.

Conditions for the Scholars were notorious. As pensioners, they received no breakfast or tea. Their only meal consisted of mutton and mashed potatoes, the potatoes dug in the season when they were too small to mash. The boys were so starved, in fact, they were known to prey upon each other, so that a small boy might subsist on bread and gravy alone.

The rats in the crumbling building where they lived fared much better. In the infamous Long Chamber where the boys slept—without care or supervision—rats ran rampant. It was said that the boys spent the better part of their nights hunting the creatures and skinning them for sport. Their other amusements—gambling and fighting among themselves and drinking whatever was smuggled in—were hardly more suited to gentlemen's sons. Nevertheless, that is what they did and where they learned the rudiments of a certain life. Some of London's most confirmed gamblers and heaviest drinkers had started out as King's Scholars.

Richard could not imagine how Augustus would survive in such a setting. Even though it might be the only way the boy could hope to get to Cambridge—Scholars were almost guaranteed a King's College Fellowship—he thought he must try to discourage him.

Richard had laid down his shears, unable to work with these disturbing thoughts in mind. On top of these he had begun to feel the result of yesterday's work. Every muscle in his back and shoulders ached. He urged the boy to take a rest by leaning against the fence. Then, when by its sway, it became apparent that this was not a good idea, they sat on the frozen grass instead.

The cold seeped up through Richard's thighs. But this was as nothing compared to the chill around his heart at the thought of such a gentle boy being thrust into a situation hardly better than a beasts' den.

"Do you know much about Eton?" he finally asked.

Augustus flushed and looked sideways at him, searching. "If you mean, do I know about a Scholar's life, the answer is yes, sir."

"And yet you would go?"

"I have no choice. That is the only way we can pay for my instruction. You might not realize it, but we sometimes have trouble making ends meet. That was why we were so uncommonly glad—"

Augustus broke off, and Richard was charmed by the mixture of maturity and naïveté in his words.

"—Why you were so uncommonly glad I came to buy your trees?" When Augustus blushed and nodded, Richard said, "You must not worry about being frank. I had perceived your sister's eagerness and understood it. It is quite reasonable."

A cloud descended on Augustus's face again. "Sir, you must promise me not to tell my sister about the Collegers' life. She doesn't know—She would not wish me to go if she ever knew—"

"You may count upon me," Richard assured him, relieved to hear that Selina had not set out to subject her brother to such misery on purpose. That question had lingered at the back of his mind and had disturbed him.

"And you, how did you find out?"

"My father was a Scholar," Augustus said.

Richard frowned. "Would he have wished you to endure what he did?"

Augustus hedged. "He would have wanted me to heed my sister's counsel."

"Even if she was ill-informed?"

The boy smiled at being caught in a diversion. "Perhaps not. But"—his tone turned serious—"I do wish to attend University. The vicar says I am quick enough, and this would be the only way."

Quicker than four-fifths of the boys there, Richard could warrant, and more responsible than the lot. "And yet only a few moments ago, you expressed doubts of ever being accepted."

A mask shuttered Augustus's face.

"Forgive me for prying," Richard said. "I only wish to know if I might be of service to you in this matter."

At his offer of friendship, Augustus turned quite pink at the ears.

"Thank you, sir. You are most generous. And you must not think I am not mindful of the help you've already given us. We will hate to see you go. But the questions you ask touch on subjects we do not commonly discuss."

"I see. And you do not think me a worthy recipient of your confidence?" Richard knew he should be ashamed for using such underhanded tactics, but he seemed so close to discovering the source of their worries. It still was possible he could help.

Augustus stumbled over his words, trying to repair Richard's mistaken impression. "No, not at all! It's not that! It's—Oh, well, I guess I might tell you some of it at any rate. My sister's already blurted out that much.

"The letter we received today—" he said. "Do you recall?"

Richard nodded.

"It was a reply to a request my sister had made." Augustus looked toward the house to make certain they were not being overheard. "Selina, you see, had written to the Garter to ask that we be allowed to use our ancestor's name. The name is Trevelyan. The same as the Earl of Linton, you know."

"Yes, I have heard the name." Richard suppressed a wry tone. "And *are* you related to the Earl of Linton?"

"Yes, we are. And my sister has proof, though—"

"It would appear not proof enough?"

Augustus nodded. His dark brow, which promised a darkening of his hair, was furrowed in a grown man's concern. But Augustus was much too young for this sort of worry.

"But why—" This did not explain anything, Richard thought. "Why will the Garter's refusal prevent your going to Eton as a King's Scholar? Your vicar could speak for you. You seem the perfect candidate, in fact." The whole purpose of these scholarships was to help the deserving impoverished.

Augustus hung his head.

"I'm sorry. You must pardon me if I've overstepped the bounds." Though, Richard thought, he had done that often of late.

Instead of accepting his apology, Augustus started speaking hesitantly. "There was a scandal. Involving my father at Cambridge. He lost his fellowship. It was known at Eton."

He looked up, a deep-seated discomfort spreading outwardly from his eyes. "That is why we must change our name before I apply to Eton."

"I see."

And although Richard did not know the details, he could see that the boy's case was hopeless as long as his father's name had been besmirched. The sins of the father were always visited on the son, no less in the halls of Eton and Cambridge than in social settings. It would be thought the boy might have the same proclivities as his father, if not worse, whatever those might be. And they must have been bad enough if he had been sent down. Not only sent down, but dispossessed of his fellowship.

"So you had planned to conceal the fact that your name was Payley?"

"Yes, sir," Augustus answered miserably. "But we did not want to do it. My father would have been strongly against it, for he always insisted he had done no wrong, and we were not to be ashamed. But Selina could think of no other way to get me into Cambridge."

With these last words Augustus glanced back toward the house and spied Selina.

"My sister is waving us in to dinner. You will not tell her anything I've said?"

"You have my word."

Although—Richard thought as he slowly unbent and stretched his back—he would rather ask what their father had been accused of. It was hard for him to believe that the man who had produced two such courageous children could have done anything abominable. Payley must have been a remarkable fellow, else his offspring would not have turned out so forthright. And certainly proud, to have insisted upon keeping his name if a scandal had attached to it.

Richard nearly limped into the kitchen, where Selina had stoked the fire to a roaring blaze. The table was set with her old silver. It made a curious mixture with the chipped platters containing bacon and cheese, a laborer's meal, and that perfidious cherry wine, which he saw was propped at his place.

The sight of it made Richard want to groan. Loath to appear weak, he bit back an oath as he settled himself down in his chair. It was all he could do to conceal the pain in his lower back from bending over those trees.

Augustus seemed not the least bit affected as he scurried

into his seat, all eager for food, but, of course, the boy did this sort of work every day. Same as Selina, who still managed to look radiant, even though she had been up for hours and had suffered a major disappointment.

Hard work must be good for the digestion, Richard decided as he piled bacon in heaps upon his plate. Good for the complexion, too, as he stared the length of the table at Selina. Her color heightened under his regard, but he did not pull it away. He would be gone soon, and he meant to drink his fill of such a pretty sight.

The truth was he was also loath to leave. Whether curiosity had kept him there or a desire to help or something altogether different, he did not know, but despite his aches and pains, he was not yet ready to go. He ought to be committed to Bedlam, perhaps, but he had found the physical labor spiritually rewarding. He found he enjoyed his bacon even better when it came upon a deprived palate. All his senses, in fact, seemed to have been heightened by this experience, which would explain his acute awareness of the woman sitting at the foot of the table.

Selina's breast rose and fell more rapidly whenever his gaze was upon her. He admired the generous curves he could detect beneath her modest gown. Her lashes trembled and fell against her high cheekbones. Though Richard knew of several ladies who used this movement as a device to attract men, he somehow knew that she employed it unintentionally. It did not take an experienced man about town to know that she was not used to the attention she deserved.

But, much as she deserved it, for him to give it to her would not be fair. It would be far from right under these troubled circumstances. He had not come under an alias to seduce an innocent maid.

Why, then, was he finding it so hard to refrain from doing so?

Chapter Six

Selina was having difficulty swallowing. It was hard to eat when Mr. Lint was looking at her. She couldn't be certain why he was staring in just that way. He had done so before, but never quite so obviously as now.

She was nearly sure she had washed all the muck off her face, so it couldn't be that. And she dared to hope that his comments earlier in the day, about her breeding and so forth, might rather be the cause. He *had* made rather pointed remarks about her appearance.

The temptation to blush was almost irresistible. Mr. Lint had none of the mooning airs of a lover, the way Romeo, to her infinite distress, often did. But then, Mr. Lint was nothing at all like Romeo Fancible. He was far too urbane to let his inclinations show.

She had a fleeting wish that he would make them a little more obvious. Then she took herself to task for indulging in worthless daydreams. She knew nothing at all about Mr. Lint, although he had said something today that had made her prick up her ears. He had referred to himself as a gentleman with an estate.

But, Selina's cautious nature reminded her, he also suggested you might like to marry someone else.

"Augustus"—she would not let the man's scrutiny put her out of countenance any longer—"would you pass Mr. Lint the cheese?" He had completely polished his plate, and there was nothing left on the table but a small hunk of Stilton.

Augustus complied, saying with a wink at Mr. Lint, "He wants us to call him Richard."

Richard. The sound of their visitor's name gave Selina a strange, cosy feeling inside, as if an oven had been lit deep within her bones. Then, abruptly, she recalled her upbringing, and her earlier fears came back to caution her.

"We mustn't presume to be so familiar, however," she said cordially, so as not to sound as if she were dealing him a rebuff. "We've only recently met." She felt the need to remind them all, for in many ways it seemed much longer.

Augustus laughed, and Richard joined him in a private joke.

Taken aback, Selina scolded herself for even thinking of him as Richard.

Augustus explained, "I told Richard you would not like it at all."

"It is not that I do not like it! I only see no reason for abandoning the conventions when one is hardly acquainted."

Richard was laughing at her with his eyes, which caused her to become more discomfited. A smile tugged at the corners of her mouth and would not be denied.

"There is no reason to call me Richard other than that it would oblige me greatly if you would do so," he said, gazing at her with a gentler light in his eyes.

"But why?"

He lifted one shoulder. "Let us just say that I don't care overmuch for the name Lint."

Selina chuckled and stared. She could not tell if he was teasing her or not.

"And you need not fear an equal familiarity on my

part, if such a thing would displease you," Richard promised. "I shall always call you Miss Payley, if you prefer." He seemed to be challenging her.

Ruffled, she said, "That would be nonsensical in the highest degree. If you are to be Richard, I must also be Selina." She squared her shoulders when she said this.

A quirk of his lips told her he was still amused, but he only inclined his head.

"For after all"—she raised her nose in the air—"if one is going to muck about with pigs with one, then one—"

Richard gave a hoot of laughter that was matched by Augustus. Before Selina knew what she was about, she was holding her sides and giggling along with their guffaws. She had not laughed so hard in years, had scarcely laughed at all, in truth, since their father died.

The thought of him now brought back her disappointment of the morning, the blow the Garter's letter had struck her. Was it not wonderful that Richard had been here to give her something to be glad about?

But time was getting on. She couldn't dally over her meal when there was work to be done. She shouldn't really ever dally at all.

She rose reluctantly. Richard would pick out his trees today, however few or many, and be gone.

She felt the smile fading from her face, but she bolstered it so as not to show how dismal this eventuality made her feel. "Shall we conclude our business now?" she asked overly perky.

Richard started to rise, then bent and, uttering a groan, fell back into his seat.

"What? What is it?" Selina rushed to help him and, in her concern, placed a hand upon his shoulder.

But he was already laughing at himself. "I'm afraid I'm not accustomed to this sort of exercise. Hunting and riding, yes, but not bending over trees."

"You should not have been pruning our trees." She threw a baleful glance Augustus's way. "That was not your work to do."

"You mustn't blame your brother. It was entirely my idea. You see, I—" Richard broke off as if a thought had crossed his mind.

"Yes . . ." he mused aloud, seemingly pleased. "It would be much to my advantage to prolong my stay."

"To do *what*?" Selina was conscious of a leaping in her chest. She didn't know what he meant, only that he had talked of staying.

"Yes. . . ." Richard turned his head and looked up at her, smiling. A curious gleam was in his eye. His dark hair shone, so close she could almost reach out and touch it.

All at once, Selina realized that her palm was still resting upon his shoulder. She was near enough to touch his hair, his lips, his chiseled face, if she wished.

Clearing her throat—embarrassed in a way far beyond her own experience—Selina made as if to dust off his coat. Then, as she did, she remembered that he had not taken a spill, that instead she had come around the table to search for his injury.

Feeling jesterish, she took a healthy step backward, stammering, "I am not sure what you meant, Rich—Mr.—" With an exasperated sigh, she left her sentence unfinished.

"What I meant," he said, politely ignoring her confusion, "was that my purpose in helping Augustus was to learn to prune trees. This plan of mine to start an orchard is quite recent, you understand. I know nothing at all about fruit trees. It would be better—if it would not inconvenience you greatly—if I were to stay and learn from you. Then I could instruct my own people."

"People? You have people—I mean, servants?" Selina

76

nearly squeaked over the word. Then, realizing what a fool she must sound, she tossed her head. "But, of course."

Sure that Richard would be laughing at her now, she turned away as much to keep from seeing his amusement as to conceal her own delight. "Well. . . ." She feigned to think about it. "No-o-o." She shot him a glance for his reaction, but Richard was sitting in his chair as confidently as before.

"No-o-o," she said again, drawing out that one syllable. "It would not be *too* great an inconvenience. I suppose you would be willing to lend us a hand about the Grange? By way of recompense for teaching you?"

Richard inclined his head. "Indeed."

"It would be like"—Selina warmed to the topic—"it would be rather like an apprenticeship!"

She nearly giggled at the struck look upon his face.

"Rather like," he said, less cocksure now.

"Then, it is agreed." Selina extended her hand to seal their bargain.

Richard had fully regained his composure now. He stood, and taking her hand in his, bowed over it, pausing long enough for Selina to wonder if he might kiss it again. Breathlessly she waited.

But something seemed to make him change his mind. He straightened his back with all trace of amusement gone.

"I had forgotten," he said grimacing, "just how much it hurts to bend."

"Oh!" She covered her mouth. "You needn't bow, you know. I do not require it."

"No, I know you don't." Richard grinned, so she could not take any offense at his next words. "You are a most extraordinary girl."

While this comment flustered her, she recovered sufficiently to agree that it would be best if he did not undertake any more work today. Richard promised to be at the Grange bright and early next morning when he supposed his soreness would be diminished.

Selina watched him depart, her heart all in turmoil, her pulse beating in irregular waves.

He was going to stay. For how long . . . to do what, she did not know, just as she had no idea where he came from.

All she knew was that he was handsome and charming and amusing and *rich*. And to top it all off, he was tall!

Richard had no trouble drifting off that night in spite of his aches and pains. The country air was good for him. It made his whole body tingle. Or, at least . . . being with Selina did.

So did thinking about her. And if all he did was think, he reasoned he could sleep with a clear conscience, for he had managed to stop himself from kissing her hand.

He slept the sleep of the dead, until a vague noise from downstairs made him turn over in bed. Another sound, and he opened his heavy eyelids. A series of muffled shouts, and he was on his feet.

He pulled on his breeches and boots, threw a shirt over his chest, and went to investigate.

Someone was making a frightful row in the taproom. As soon as Richard entered, he spied who it was.

Lucas. That master of all trades, that bulwark, that prop, who was holding the Payleys up by the grace of God, was far more than three sheets to the wind. He was staggering and swearing, and looping drunk. He was—to put it like a Colonial—smashed.

Clenching his jaw, Richard approached the wrangling pair—Lucas, who seemed to have forgotten where he was, and poor Mr. Croft, who was protecting his tankards from being tossed about.

"How long has he been like this?" Richard asked, collaring the culprit.

"Too long, sir." Mr. Croft wiped his forehead upon his sleeve, seemingly grateful for the intervention. "I've been trying to get him to leave. I don't want the constable down upon my house.

He bent to shout into Lucas's deaf ears. "Go on home, ye fool! Ye see what ye've done? Ye've roused m' best customer."

Lucas twisted his neck to give Richard a searching look. "Never seen 'un," he mumbled. "Don' know this 'un."

"Yes, ye do, ye ass." Mr. Croft hunched a shoulder Richard's way. "This here's the swell that's been up t' the Grange these past two days."

Mr. Croft turned to Richard and spoke in a confidential tone, "You'll forgive me, sir, for speaking o' ye like that, but this'un's such a fool, he don't understand anything else."

"Not at all," Richard said, and indeed, if he had seemed taken aback, it was only because the knowledge that he had spent but two days in Uckfield had surprised him so. It seemed like years.

Not in a negative way, except for his aching back. It was rather that he felt he had known the pair at the Grange for many weeks, so fast had their intimacy grown. He felt he knew them better than he did any gentleman in his London clubs.

But, with Lucas struggling to free himself, this was not the moment for such reflections. He must be dealt with at once. Richard did not want him to cause trouble for the Payleys.

"If he has broken anything," Richard said, holding on while Lucas swung his arms in futile circles, "you may put it on my bill."

Mr. Croft seemed stunned. "Ye needn't pay for anything, Mr. Lint. I'd be dashed before I'd dun the squire.

"Besides"—he shrugged—"Lucas does the same nearly once a fortnight. Every time Miss Selina pays him a bit."

Richard ignored the last part of Mr. Croft's speech long enough to note his generosity. It was clear that his declining to charge the Payleys stemmed from affection and respect. They might not have been so fortunate, and he found himself comforted by the knowledge that they were.

"Well," he said, absorbing the last bit of Mr. Croft's speech as well, "if this is a common occurrence, what do you normally do with him?"

"I gets 'im home. Either me or one of the neighbors."

Richard thought, and quickly decided. "Would you like me to take him?"

Mr. Croft stared with a question behind his eyes, but Richard could see he had welcomed the offer.

"I do not care for the thought of burdening Miss Payley with him at this hour, no matter how often she has been before," Richard said to explain himself.

Mr. Croft cocked a speculative brow his way. "That's the right of it, sir, as I've been saying to the wife many a time this past two year. It's time Miss Selina had some help about the place. And I mean," he said in a weighted tone, "sommat more than just another hand.

"She needs a good husband to take the load off her back. And the Grange"—Mr. Croft gave him an ingenuous wink—"you might not think much about it, seeing as how it's looking a bit rough about the edges, but it's a fine piece of property, sir. Them cherries she grows, they'll—"

Getting the drift of Mr. Croft's meaning, Richard decided to cut him off, no matter how well-intentioned his remarks. "That's quite all right. Now, if you will be so good as to harness up your cart, I shall unburden myself of this—"

Seeing that Richard meant to throw Lucas over his shoulder, Mr. Croft rushed to hold the door, and Richard was not obliged to finish his sentence. Not that he could have finished it very well with the deadweight of a man on his back.

For as soon as Richard had heaved him, all the fight had gone out of Lucas, and Richard's back had screamed in protest.

Grunting, not so much from the weight as from his aching muscles, Richard strode bent to the yard. Afraid that once he had put Lucas down, he might not be able to lift him again, he stood and waited for Mr. Croft to hitch the horse to a cart. No doubt the beast was as resentful as Richard had been to be roused from his bed at this hour. They had both put in enough work for one day, and the beast, unlike Richard, had no ulterior motive in mind.

Or not ulterior, Richard admitted, grinning to himself, for the promise of seeing Selina in her wrapper—a sleepy, grateful Selina—was very much at the forefront of his brain.

And he was not disappointed. When he arrived at the Grange, his loud knocks roused her, and she came rushing down in an ancient negligee clasped about her sleeping garb. Her rich brown hair hung loose down her back, falling almost to her waist. The anxious expression with which she opened the door vanished from her face as soon as she spied Richard under his burden.

"Richard!" she cried, her voice full of shock.

No "Mr. Lint" this time, he noted with satisfaction. She must have been thinking of him to change her habits so soon.

"What are you doing with Lucas?"

"Retrieving him, like a good hunting dog." He was beginning to feel like a dog all bent over at the waist. "Where do you wish me to put him?"

She backed, saying quickly, "His room is on the second floor, but you must not—"

"Show me the way." Not lingering for her directions, Richard headed for the stairs, eager to make the two flights and drop the body.

Making the slow but steady progress of an overloaded cart, Richard could hear Selina skipping nervously in his wake. Her anxious flutterings to left and right behind him brought a smile to his lips, just as the knowledge that he was alone with her heated his blood. He had not disturbed Augustus with his knock, nor was Lucas in any shape to act as chaperon.

"You should put him down. Just put him here on the stairs, and he can waken in the morning and get himself into bed. Richard"—Selina skipped to the other side, but his bulk still blocked her way—"can you hear me? I insist that you put him down at once. I should thrash him— and I shall thrash him soundly for causing you this inconvenience. Lucas, you are worse than Nero!"

This tirade went on until he reached the first landing and interrupted her. "Where are the servants' stairs?"

"They are down the hall to your left, but you will oblige me very much if you will put him down here at once."

"And litter your stairs?" Richard turned left and proceeded on his way. "Leave him for someone to trip over? I don't think that would be wise."

"And, pray, who would trip over him? I am not running a hotel. Richard, I think you are ignoring me."

"Not at all." He cast a glance back at her under his arm, but his burden shifted and he nearly lost it. "I am enjoying your company far too much. But you would be even more useful, if you could spring ahead and open his door."

At the second landing, Richard pressed himself aside so Selina could squeeze past him. She did so, muttering under her breath, ". . . more stubborn than Caesar . . ."

Selina's grumbling left him grinning from ear to ear, even though he had not found her more docile in the night. He ought to have known better, he told himself. But at least she had compared him to the bull and not the pig.

And she was doing as he'd requested long enough to push open the rickety door at the end of the corridor and to turn back Lucas's covers.

With a grunt of relief, Richard heaved the deadweight off his shoulder and onto the bed. Lucas's head flopped down onto the pillow. His mouth fell open, and he snored.

"Well, I am certainly glad you are getting such a good night's sleep"—Selina's angry voice came from the foot of the bed—"I am sure Mr. Lint would be devastated to think he had disturbed your peace."

Richard straightened his back, taking care not to wrench it with a sudden motion. Finding his aching muscles no better than they should be, he came up slowly. But, as he turned and found her struggling to take off Lucas's boots, he quickly intervened.

"Why not leave that to me?" he said, taking her by the shoulders and urging her gently toward the door.

"But I always put him to bed when he comes home like this."

Richard could see that she would not relinquish her responsibility unless he gave her something else to do. He refrained from kissing her, which had been his first impulse on touching her thusly, and said regretfully instead,

"Why do you not go down to the kitchen and put a kettle on for tea. I find I could use a cup."

"Your poor back," Selina recalled, a sympathetic look disturbing her lovely face. "Does it hurt too dreadfully?"

"No." What hurt most at the moment was not his back, but Richard reprimanded himself. He had let a momentary fantasy run away with him. "I find that carrying a snoring corpse up two flights of stairs has done wonders for my spine."

The look of confusion she gave him was almost too much for his resistance, but he turned her toward the stairs and gave her another gentle push. "I shall join you in a moment."

Closing the door with a determined sigh, he reminded himself of his duplicity. It would be the height of dishonor to take advantage of a helpless maid, and Selina, for all her bravery and capability, was helpless in that respect. Still, for all his self-confessed hopes, he had not realized that the sight of her in her night rail would drive him to quite this level of desire.

The smell of stale gin recalled him to his present task, and woke him to the squalor of Lucas's room, which was littered with unlaundered garments. It appeared the man was as much a sloth in his personal habits as he was on the job.

Feeling much more fastidious than he had when dealing with Nero, Richard quickly relieved Lucas of his boots, then pulled the coverlets over him. Whether deserved or not, the cold could not be allowed to sicken him.

A few minutes later, Richard found Selina in the kitchen with the fire warmly stoked and a kettle put on to boil. He was not used to drinking tea at this hour and would have preferred a nip of brandy instead, but he hoped he had forestalled the offer of a glass of cherry wine.

Selina had had time to recover from her anger and to

let modesty intrude. She greeted him shyly, her long lashes cloaking the embarrassment in her eyes.

If Richard had thought that Selina aroused was like a blow to his chest, he discovered now how great a kick she delivered when shy. The warm firelight bathed her in its gentle glow. It was all Richard could do not to cross the room and take her into his arms.

Fighting this improper thought, which must be carefully analyzed before it ruled his behavior, he turned his back to the fire, welcoming its heat on his aching muscles.

"I have some liniment, if you. . . ."

"No—" he nearly choked at the image her words had raised, even though he knew it to be the result of false hopes. Selina was not offering to apply the liniment herself.

"No, thank you, I am perfectly fine," he said. "I shall not be staying long, just a minute to catch my breath."

"I should thank you, I know, for troubling yourself over Lucas, but you truly should not. Mr. Croft would have taken care of him."

"I know. He was ready to do so until I offered to take his place."

"You did?" Selina whispered softly. "You have been very kind. Much too kind."

"No, I haven't." As Richard waved her gratitude away, he decided he had best give in to his grievances than to his more pressing desires. "I have done what any gentleman would do when faced with the evidence of your distress.

"I cannot imagine," he continued irritably, "why you would put up with such a wastrel as Lucas, when you need a much more capable servant."

Selina's chin jerked up. "I put up with him because at least he will do some of what I need, and there is no one else around."

"No one else? You mean, no one better to employ?" He shook his head. "I cannot believe that. I'm afraid you have given in to pity. You keep him on for fear of what will become of him."

"No, you are wrong." He had truly raised her ire now, as her flashing eyes told him. "The reason I keep him has nothing at all to do with pity. I would abandon him in a trice if I could afford anyone else." The force of her words seemed to take her aback. She lowered her eyes. "Well, perhaps not that quickly. But it is true that I would prefer practically anyone to Lucas.

"You see," she admitted with a twist to her lips, "I cannot truly afford to pay anyone at all, although I can feed Lucas and give him a roof over his head, which no one else seems willing to do. And, in exchange, I at least get some work out of him, as well as the appearance of having a servant, which lends us propriety."

The very notion that Lucas might lend propriety to such a fine lady made Richard balk. "You should get far more from him than that. And I doubt that you need his chaperonage, if that is what you mean by propriety, when you have the deep respect of the entire village."

Selina's expression softened. Her eyes filled, and her lips, if Richard could only taste them, plumped like luscious fruit. "The villagers have been kind. They refuse to accept that we have lost whatever respect our family once deserved."

"You mustn't speak like that. Not in my hearing." Now Richard was angry. With Selina for saying such things, and with himself for being so powerless to help her. "You deserve far more than they give you."

"Why?"

"For going it alone. For facing every day as bravely as a soldier. A most beautiful soldier at that . . ."

Selina blushed, and he bit back further words. *Get a*

grip on yourself, Richard, he told himself. Stop interjecting worthless compliments.

If he were not careful, he would frighten Selina into silence, and above all, he wanted to know more so he could help her.

Changing the subject abruptly, he said, "Augustus spoke of his hopes of going to Eton and Cambridge."

She turned away and noisily cleared her throat. "Yes, he is a bright student. The vicar insists he will do well as a Scholar."

"Yet Augustus tells me there is some impediment to his being accepted."

There. It was better to come out with it directly than to beat about the bush any longer.

Selina had turned a paler shade under his assault, and Richard admitted to himself there had been something confrontational about his tone.

"Yes," she said, meeting his gaze head-on with a proud glance. "My father was accused of cheating at cards when he was at Cambridge." She waited for his reaction, but when none was forthcoming, she went on, "The matter was never resolved, and, so he was expelled. Unfortunately his masters at Eton were informed. Mr. Newman, our vicar, says it will be useless for Augustus to apply under his name."

It had been easy for Richard to keep a bland expression, for he had suspected something as bad as this. All he cared about at the moment was that she had trusted him enough to tell him about her father's disgrace.

Unless, he reminded himself, she simply could not withstand his challenge to her pride, which was more than likely.

"Which is why you applied to take the name Trevelyan," he remarked.

Selina started. Her eyes grew round. Richard felt a breath of suspicion drifting past the nape of his neck.

"I did not think I had mentioned any name," she said.

Chapter Seven

Selina stared at Richard, who seemed to have frozen. He blinked once, then twice, before he finally said, "Yes, you did. Though earlier, when I first arrived. You presented yourself as Selina Trevelyan."

His tone was perfectly firm, but Selina could have sworn something had discomfited him. Distracted by more pressing concerns, she waved that thought away.

"So I did," she admitted ruefully. "And it seems I did so very foolishly, as things turn out, for our application was denied."

Richard stared at her silently. Long enough for Selina to fear she had disgusted him with her troubles. She ought never to have blurted them out, but the truth was she had half wondered how he would react to her father's story. Would he be quick to turn his back on them both?

Her heart beat stronger as he took a step nearer. She could feel the comforting warmth of his presence.

"Augustus is a fine chap," Richard said. His strangely hesitant note seemed to make the air move between them. "Much more deserving than half the boys at Eton. Is there anything I can do to see that he succeeds?"

His offer poured warmth inside her, like a strong cup of tea spreading swiftly through her veins. It weakened her at the knees, making her long to lay all her troubles before him.

But that would be a mistake. She could not inflict all her woes upon a man, even so kind a man as Richard, without running him off.

And, she remembered suddenly, she had forgotten entirely about his tea.

Tossing him a flustered smile, she hurried past him and swept the boiling kettle from the fire. He seemed taken aback, until he saw what she was about and insisted on taking the heavy kettle from her hands as if she did not lift things far bigger than that every day.

Pouring the water into the pot she held for him, Richard frowned, deep in thought. This shared task brought their heads together. From no more than a foot away, Selina studied the light flickering over his sculpted features, the glint of its reflection in his dark, wavy hair, the strong curve of his lips. A tingling sensation, as if the world were trembling beneath her feet, made her rock toward him.

All at once, he seemed aware of her scrutiny. His eyes met hers.

The gleam in their blue depths threatened to take her breath away.

His emboldened gaze fell to the front of her night rail. Selina felt a responsive surge before she recalled, with a rush of shame, how grossly improper this all was.

She quickly turned away and bustled about the room, noisily fetching cups and saucers and milk. Richard was watching her. She could feel his gaze between her shoulder blades. She could almost imagine the fun that would be in his eyes; but then he cleared his throat—a sound of strangulation, not amusement—and she dared hope he had been as unsettled by their proximity as she had.

"You were about"— he spoke firmly behind her—"to tell me what I could do to help."

She threw him a challenging glance. "I was?"

He grinned and nodded.

Just one look at his grin, and Selina knew the truth. More than anything else on earth, she did want this man to share her troubles.

"I—" she faltered under the enormity of that thought. "You are very kind, but I—"

"Why do you not tell me the basis for your claim?" he suggested gently. "Perhaps, on a legal issue such as that, I might be able to shed some light."

Yes. Of course. Selina wondered that she hadn't thought of this herself. With so little money to support them, she had not dared to seek the advice of a solicitor, but Richard might well know more than she about matters of the law.

He might even *be* a solicitor, for all she knew.

Dismissing this notion as highly unlikely, she nodded her agreement and stepped over to her mother's chest.

Richard waited in suspense while she searched its contents. At last he would see what he had come for. He was surprised when she returned with nothing more than a faded scrap of blue paper. Selina handed it to him, and he glanced at it no more than a second before raising his eyes.

"A valentine?" he said, unable to hide his astonishment.

His incredulous tone made her flush. "Yes, but see what it says." She moved to his side.

Holding her wrapper tightly about her, she pointed to the words on the worn piece of paper. "Read the message," she urged him.

Reluctantly tearing his gaze from her face, Richard returned it to the faded page with the silvered edges. The valentine had been written in the quaint style of another century. A pair of hand-painted swans, their necks drawn to meet in the shape of a heart, graced the top of the page.

Yellow stains of age had spread over the words, but he could still make them out.

Turning to let the firelight spill over them, he read aloud,

> "Moste suitors chouse theyr love by chance,
> Yet, I disdayne to follow such a dance,
> But take my wisdome from the birds above,
> To plight my troth in steade to truest love,
> That this won yeere shall turn to lyfe.
> When Valentyne shalle bee my wyfe."

Finishing, Richard turned over the paper to see how it had been directed. In a flowing hand he read, "To Mistress Anne Trevellian" and the signature of the sender, "Mr. Joshua Payley, Esquire."

Feeling Selina's eager gaze upon him, he raised his own eyes. "Where did you come by this?" he asked.

"It was among the few belongings my father brought from his parents' house. It had been tucked away inside a small volume of Milton's poetry, which was published in 1645. My father received it as a gift from his father and took it with him to Cambridge."

Her gaze faltered. "It is the only piece of family history Augustus and I have. My uncle, who never speaks to us, has the rest of the family papers. My father never did return home from Cambridge. He was not received."

"And you think the book had been in your family for many years?"

Selina nodded, her face filling again with hope. "I know it had. My father said that was the significance of the gift."

Richard looked down at the valentine again and felt a wave of conflicting emotions. Sympathy warred with his common sense.

"Do you attach any significance to the fact that it had been so preserved?"

"No." Selina's calm voice reassured him that she had not imagined some improbable, Gothic plot. "I think it had been overlooked for years. For more than one hundred years."

He raised his head at that.

"If you'll remember"—the glow of eagerness lit Selina's face—"Cromwell forbade the practice of any custom he considered pagan in origin. Choosing valentines was one of these, yet we know that such laws were never strictly obeyed. The common people are not easily discouraged from having their celebrations, and the gentry usually follow suit. Still, Cromwell's rule was so severe, they would have hidden any evidence of their crimes."

"So," Richard said, "you are supposing that the valentine was hidden in a book and only came to your father by chance?"

"Yes. But Papa took little interest in keeping it. My mother was the one who found something in it to cherish. She said it meant that our ancestor Mr. Joshua Payley had married Miss Anne Trevelyan."

"But"—Richard did not want to discourage her, but he had to make her see sense—"but how could she be so certain? I know the message speaks of marriage, but that does not mean they ever wed."

The light in Selina's eyes flickered. "Mama told me that, more often than not, valentines used to marry at the end of the year. Just as the verse says."

"I know, I know. But, dear girl, surely not all valentines would marry. Such a custom imposes no strict adherence. What is to say that this is anything more than a whim on your ancestor's part?"

"A whim?" Selina's color was rising. "He hardly

employs the tone of a whim. Look again"—she leaned closer, jabbing at the words with her first finger—"he speaks of her as his truest love." Her tone softened as her fingers drifted over the swans. "And, see here. He painted swans, which are known to mate for life. How can you miss the significance?"

Richard had not missed the significance, but right now, he was more than a little distracted by Selina's closeness.

The age-softened lace on her wrapper was tickling the back of his hand. Her shoulder was pressed against his, and her touch warmed him from neck to toe. As he breathed in her sweet scent, desire swept the length of his body.

He closed his eyes and tried to focus on her question, but the urge to make love to her had much too firm a hold. He struggled with his wishes. The last thing he should do would be to take advantage of a girl in her position. Alone at night.

"Richard?" Her questioning tone brought him back to the problem at hand.

He stammered, "I—I quite see where you are leading, but you still have no proof that his love was returned."

Selina smiled, and the wistfulness behind that smile nearly proved his undoing. "What girl could refuse such a lover? He sends her poetry. He pledges his undying love. He braves Cromwell's wrath to send her a forbidden valentine. And . . ." Selina paused long enough for a dimple to punctuate her cheek. " . . . And besides. He was a Payley."

Richard answered with a grin of his own, though he longed to hold Selina instead. He wanted to plant a kiss in the hollow of her cheek to see what that dimple would feel like. He wanted to loosen the ribbons from about her lovely neck and slowly watch the night rail fall from her magnificent shoulders. He wanted to forget who he was long enough to drink his fill of her.

All of this he wanted, but his hands were paralyzed by the deceit he had practiced upon her. By that, and by his native caution.

He wanted her as much as he'd ever wanted a woman, more in fact than any other to date, but what did this girl mean to him?

He couldn't be sure yet, but he did know one thing. Selina Payley did not deserve to be trifled with. And if he did not know where he wished to lead her, he would have to keep hands off.

"Selina—" He yanked his mind back to the issue at hand. "I have no wish to discourage you. Truthfully I do not." And he had found he did not. "But surely you must see why the Garter had to refuse your request? Even if this valentine is to be believed, it links your family and—and the family of Trevelyan through the female line."

"There is precedence for taking the name of a female ancestor," she said stubbornly.

"Yes, but the evidence—You must know a valentine is not a legal document."

"Yes, but—" As she stammered, all the fight seemed to leave her. The light in her eyes had dimmed. "Why can he not search to see whether a more solid piece of evidence exists? That is all I ask. This valentine"—she caressed the bit of paper in his hand—"is the only thing I have."

Richard watched her hand moving over the faded paper so lovingly, and his desire rose to a fever pitch. To stop himself from acting rashly, he cleared his throat, which made her suddenly stop.

Seemingly aware for the first time of their close proximity, she inched her hand away from his—as if by inching she could evade his notice—then her shoulder and her hip. When they were no longer touching, Richard turned, to place another few important inches between them. With his gaze awkwardly averted, he handed her back the family relic.

Closing her wrapper more snugly about her now, Selina returned the valentine to her mother's chest, which gave Richard time to draw a deep, restraining breath.

"I had best get back to the inn, or Mr. Croft will wonder what I've been doing."

As Selina's head came up, her startled look quickly changing to a blush, Richard wished he had used a more felicitous turn of phrase. He had not meant to imply what he had implied, but the truth was, Mr. Croft might be ready to jump to certain conclusions. Richard had stayed much longer than he ought. Certainly long enough to . . .

With an effort he diverted his mind from such wishful thinking, and drew himself up stiffly. Selina seemed to misinterpret his motion, for she raised her chin in the air.

"I will show you to the door. Thank you again, Mr. Lint, for bringing Lucas home."

She turned her back with a swish of her long, lustrous hair, making Richard feel like the blackguard he knew he was.

If she only knew what restraint he had shown. . . .

However, at the sight of that back, so slim and strong, he knew he could not leave her like this. Had he not asked how he might help?

"Selina . . ." He placed a hand upon her shoulder to turn her. As she faced him, he kept it there, and his other came to rest in a similar place. "I would like to help you. Truly, I would. . . ."

But as she gazed up at him with wide-open eyes, he wondered what he could do. What could he do to strengthen her application?

Richard admitted he would be pleased to acknowledge her and Augustus as members of his family. A man could do much worse than to have these two claiming kinship with him. Why, when he thought of Wilfrid . . .

At the thought of Wilfrid, a notion did enter his head. The last time he had seen his cousin, Wilfrid had been eager to do something to make up for his most recent sins. He had been quite contrite . . . for Wilfrid, and anxious to prove his attachment to the Trevelyan family.

"Selina," Richard began again, enjoying the warmth of her shoulders beneath his palms. "Would you have any idea where your Payley ancestors came from?"

She gave her head a little shake, as if her mind had wandered. "Of course. They come from Cuckfield."

"Cuckfield? You mean here?"

"No." She smiled, and her delightful dimples peeped at him again. "Cuckfield. This is Uckfield, remember?"

"Yes, of course." Now it was Richard's turn to shake his head, but the truth was his mind was fogged by the soft feel of her beneath his hands. She had not stepped back, as she might have, but had taken a step closer as if to search his face for his intent. His hands, of their own volition, had begun to stroke her back. He willed them to stop, but he could not bring himself to remove them entirely.

"Then . . . where is Cuckfield?" he said, trying to keep the two names straight in his brain.

"It is west of here, still in Sussex, but across the Heath."

"Near the Brighton Road?"

"I think so." She flushed a warm, rosy color. "I am ashamed to admit it, but I never have been so far from home."

Oh, do not blush, dear, Richard begged her silently as the warmth of her color rushed through him. *You are much too tempting when you blush.*

He cleared his throat again and said aloud, "And how long would the Payleys have lived in that region?"

"Forever, I should suppose."

"Then, there must be record of their marriages in a church near Cuckfield." His voice was growing husky; he could barely think. "A marriage between Anne Trevelyan and Joshua Payley might be found."

Selina's face lit, then clouded over immediately. "Yes, but I cannot leave the Grange to go in search of them. I had hoped the Garter might instigate a search—"

Richard interrupted her with a shake of his head. "No, it will be up to you to produce the relevant documents."

"But I cannot leave the Grange! If I do, who will milk Clarissa and feed Nero and keep Caesar out of my garden—"

"Hold on, hold on!" Richard chuckled at her increasing frustration. She was so beautiful in a temper, he might have provoked her on purpose just to see the result, but he preferred to comfort her instead.

And somehow, with that soothing, his hands had slipped down her back and he was holding her within the circle of his arms. Lowering her lashes, she placed her palms upon his chest.

Richard suppressed a groan. He was going to kiss her, unless he could think of something to prevent himself. The brush of her negligee against his breeches was driving him mad.

Wilfrid. Think of Wilfrid, he told himself, rubbing the tops of her arms. Then, once more master of himself, he held her away, trying to ignore the puzzled look his motion aroused.

"I have a cousin," he said over the desire trapped in his throat. "A cousin who resides in Brighton. I could write to him and ask him to search for such a listing."

His offer temporarily wiped the hint of injury from her expression, leaving a frown in its place.

"But will he be willing to undertake such a mission for someone he does not know?"

Richard grinned, for once quite sure of where he stood. Since he paid Wilfrid an allowance, his cousin was at his beck and call. "Yes, never fear. He is in my debt, so to speak. The last time we had words, he assured me of his eagerness to do me any service."

Or perhaps not any service, Richard corrected himself. Nothing would persuade Wilfrid to lead a more disciplined life.

Selina's eyes turned a deeper shade of brown as she searched his face with concern. "Are you quite certain?" A note of hope had entered her voice.

"Quite, quite certain," he told her, raising one finger to wipe away her frown. The brush of her eyebrows against his fingertips aroused him as no other woman's kisses ever had.

Was it the country air that made his desire for her so overwhelming, or was it something more?

Feeling unable to sort out his feelings—not with guilt so prominent among them—he reluctantly let go of her. Before relinquishing her entirely, though, his hands lightly swept the length of her arms.

Richard could see by the hurt in her eyes that his actions had confused her, but he could not explain himself until he knew his own mind. Richard wished that he could kick himself, but the laws of physics would make that extremely difficult. He would have to devise a different punishment for himself, but that ought to be easy, since it would be sheer torture to work alongside Selina for the next week—or weeks—without touching her.

"I shall write my cousin in the morning," he said, half turning away. "Then, I shall stay until he reports to make sure there is nothing else I can do."

Her voice shook as she responded, "That would be very kind of you. You've been—"

Richard cut her off with a raised hand. "Please, don't

say it. Every moment I've been here has been a pure delight."

He could not regret this admission, for his words did something to erase the hurt in her eyes. A wavering smile touched her lips as she bid him good night.

Selina showed Richard out, still smarting from his withdrawal. She had been so sure, so certain, that he was going to kiss her.

Her pulse was still jumping like a kettle aboil, and now it threatened to explode. How and why, and how dare he stop holding her when he did?

Selina tried to put the whole incident out of her mind to focus on the assistance he had promised her instead, but her treacherous heart kept returning to the feel of his palms upon her back. His large palms. His warm, pressing palms, which had awakened a fierce longing deep inside her.

How dare he? How dare he brush her brows with his fingers, leaving the hint of a kiss in their wake?

How dare he rub against her like a tomcat wishing to be petted, then jerk away as if he meant only to tease?

Selina reached for his cup and saucer intending to slam them in the bucket to wash, only to find that the cup had not been used. She had forgotten to pour his tea.

A wave of mortification swept over her. That had been it. That had certainly been the reason he had changed so suddenly before her eyes.

He had decided that she was not good enough for him to kiss because she had the manners of a peasant. Or worse—she gripped his cup tighter—he had thought that any girl who neglected her guest's comfort while attempting to seduce him in her mother's wrapper was no better than she should be.

A wave of tears threatened. Selina fought them off

with an angry pass at her cheek. Richard had misread her. She would never have so forgotten herself as to . . .

A wish for a kiss did not amount to a seduction, even if she had forgotten about his tea.

Leaving the cups and saucers and milk and the brimming pot of tea until morning, she took the stairs to her room, remembering at once her last journey this way.

The sight of Richard carrying a man over his shoulder as if he were a featherweight had made her stomach flutter. She was ashamed to recall her wayward thoughts at that moment, for her brain had sprung to the conclusion that if he could carry a man so easily, he might carry her just as well.

"So would Romeo," she said now, giving each step an angry stomp, "and yet you have never let him put you in such a dither."

No. And she had never wanted Romeo to kiss her or even to hold her hand. Selina admitted that all she felt upon seeing Romeo Fancible was a strong desire to hide, just as she cringed whenever he opened his mouth.

But not so with Richard. Every day he had spent at the Grange had seemed the best of her life. He had hardly spoken before she had cast her heart at his feet. And even now, when he had trod upon it—softly to be sure, but still he had trod—even now she ached to see him tomorrow.

At the thought of facing him, Selina uttered a groan. She reached the head of the stairs and hurried to her bed to burrow under the covers. She still was shivering from the excitement of his touch, the warm look in his eyes, his gaze at her lips as he'd brushed the frown from her forehead.

She *had not* imagined those things. She felt a leap of hope. How could she have imagined a look she had never seen before?

But if Richard was attracted to her in the least, why had he suddenly left without saying a word of what was in his heart?

Selina pounded the pillows on her bed, frustrated by her lack of experience. If she had ever lived in town, had ever entertained gentlemen suitors, she would probably be much more capable of judging masculine thoughts. As it was, she had nothing to go on but that certain look Caesar got in his eyes when Clarissa spurred his interest, for certainly Richard would not bellow in pursuit the way Caesar did, giving all away. And she thought she had glimpsed something of that look tonight.

She mused until the nature of her thoughts made her reel in disgust. How could she be so coarse as to compare any gentleman to a bull? What would Richard think of her if he knew? That she was a peasant, and he had been right to hold her off.

"Well, let him think that," she muttered. "Let him think whatever he wants. And if he believes me unworthy of him, I will show him who's unworthy until he cries aloud for mercy!"

But such vengeful thoughts gave her little comfort as she cried herself to sleep.

Chapter Eight

The next morning, Richard sought out paper and ink from Mrs. Croft and penned a letter to Wilfrid.

It gave him immense satisfaction to call his cousin to duty, for Wilfrid would not dare to ignore his summons. Richard only wished he could see the look on his cousin's face when he received it.

Since Wilfrid had already been privy to the letter from the Garter, Richard saw no reason to be overly discreet. He certainly had no intention of divulging either the circumstances under which he had been living in Uckfield or his strange reasons for maintaining an alias. Considering, however, the extreme umbrage Wilfrid had taken at the notion that "mere husbandmen" would claim kinship with him, Richard could not stop himself from rubbing a little salt into his wounds.

He wrote Wilfrid that upon investigation he had learned that some relationship might indeed exist between the Payleys and the Trevelyans. Due to factors Richard would not trouble his cousin with, he had taken it upon himself to confirm the evidence of a marriage that was supposed to have taken place. In consideration of Wilfrid's moving testament of his devotion to their family, so recently given, Richard thought it only right to entrust a portion of the task to him.

Richard asked him without delay—saving the Regent's

extreme displeasure—to proceed to a small village by the name of Cuckfield off the Brighton Road, and once there, to search the church registries within a reasonable distance. The devil inside Richard prompted him to suggest that a radius of twenty miles ought to be more than sufficient. He gave Wilfrid a probable range of dates, but told him not to feel constrained if he found a more extensive search was warranted. If either family name was unearthed in a particular church, Wilfrid might think about rummaging in the churchyard for a joint burial spot.

Richard wrote instructions to send all evidence of his discoveries to a Mr. Lint in care of the inn at Uckfield.

He added this final note: he made no doubt his cousin would reap his due reward for exerting himself in such a worthy cause. He remained his loving servant, Richard, Earl of Linton, etcetera, and so forth. . . .

While scribbling this last, Richard chuckled to himself, knowing how galled Wilfrid would be. To have to leave Brighton with Prinny in residence to go traipsing about the countryside, poking in ice-cold churches and musty records, and on Richard's behalf, would likely make him froth at the mouth. Richard could almost hear Wilfrid's complaints, which he was sure to be treated to at length upon their next encounter.

This vision of Wilfrid incommoded made Richard almost forget what he was about. Before he considered his actions fully, he had almost franked his letter. He stopped himself in time, then had to cross through the portion of his signature already formed, for it would not do for the Crofts to be apprised of his identity. Wilfrid would be obliged to pay the postage, which fact could only increase Richard's mirth.

By the time he left for the Grange, riding his own horse to give it much-needed exercise, he was in a capital humor. Selina would be waiting to hear what he had done, and her gratitude would know no bounds. Richard wondered what form her thanks would take; however, remembering what his restraint had cost him the night before, he was not sure how much longer he could resist her. The prospect of having to take defensive measures was positively delicious.

Expecting, then, upon arriving, to receive a wide smile of welcome, he was taken aback to find a distinct coolness in Selina's manner. She seemed much too busy to give him a penny's worth of her attention today. Though civil—almost noxiously so—she obviously felt none of the emotions he had expected her to feel. She acknowledged the report on his letter with a regal incline of her head, thanked him with frigid politeness, then proceeded to assign him his day's tasks.

Since these included some backbreaking work—digging up the stumps of dead trees to make room for new ones and splitting branches for firewood—Richard was none too pleased. He had offered to stay in the hope of sparing her a portion of labor, which he admitted he would be doing. But he had never in his wildest dreams expected to be submitted to such degrading work as this.

And with no one but Lucas for a helpmate. Not Selina. Not even Augustus. But the laziest man it had ever been his lot to know.

Richard could only marvel at Lucas's talents for avoiding work. If a tool was called for, he had to spend an hour honing its edge while Richard did all the groundwork. If a stump proved difficult, then Lucas developed an ache or pain to incapacitate him for the length of time it took Richard to extract the roots from the ground.

And all the while, the scapegrace had the nerve to give directions on how the work should be done, considering himself something of an expert in the field. Richard thought he could take the work, and quite readily perform it if Selina were beside him, but, after a few hours of this abuse, he thought he would much rather be damned.

Her words of the day before came back to haunt him, some nonsense about being her apprentice. The Earl of Linton, an apprentice? For Christ's sake, what would his ancestors have to say? He had not taken her words seriously, even though for a moment they had given him pause.

All he had meant to do was hang about until her claim was proven or not. And then . . .

Yes, that was the rub, and no mistaking it, Richard admitted. And then, pray tell, what?

If the Payleys were proven to be related to him, then he might force his charity upon them. It was his duty as the head of the clan to care for his dependents. And nothing would give him more pleasure than to extend his protection to Selina and her brother . . . if they would have it.

But his reward for these noble intentions—even if Selina remained innocently unaware of them—had been this. Complete and utter relegation to the rank of common laborer.

Despite his increasing sense of ill-use, Richard was not one to quit, so he stayed at his job until the dinner bell rang. Something was surely wrong when Selina would not even come to invite him to dine in a civilized manner.

Richard returned his heavy tools to the barn, not intending to take them up again that day. After a few words with Selina, he expected his regimen would change.

He found her in the kitchen, calmly stirring a pot over the fire, as if she'd been standing by it all day. He had scarcely seen her that morning, save when she'd greeted him and assigned him his chores. He had thought then that she somehow looked different, but her cool welcome had wiped such considerations from his mind. Now he noticed this again and searched for the cause.

The only difference he could see was that she had worn the yellow ribbons in her hair again. Whether these were what gave it its incredible luster or some additional brushing, he could not know. But before he could ponder her reason for wearing them, she turned, and a look of surprise came over her face, as if she had not expected to see him.

"Oh, Richard." She gave a little laugh. "Of course, how silly of me. I shall set another place."

Her negligent greeting struck a blow to Richard's vanity. Tired as he was, he found himself responding with little grace, "You did not think I would be hungry after digging up ancient stumps all morning? Or, perhaps, you thought I might prefer to dine with Lucas?"

His sarcasm did not escape her. She flushed. But instead of apologizing as he'd expected, she paused on her way to the table, raising a finger to her chin as if to contemplate his question. "No," she finally said in a decisive tone. "I think you should eat with us. If you sit with Lucas, you might get lice."

Richard started. An itch he had not noticed before had nestled between his shoulder blades. Anxious, he arched his back, surreptitiously trying to scrape his bones together.

Selina cast him a quick glance, then turned to hide her expression from his view. Richard stopped his awkward movements, a vague suspicion entering his head.

"How kind of you," he said rather heavily, "to consider my welfare. But I would hate to foist myself upon you, if you had rather not include me."

"Oh, no." Selina's tone was quite airy again. "You are perfectly welcome to dine with Augustus and me. I daresay, we shall hardly notice you."

Hardly notice me? Distracted from his suspicions, Richard grumbled to himself. When last night you nearly melted in my arms?

For she *had* almost melted. That was what had made it so hard for him to push her away, that look of willing surrender he had seen in her deep brown eyes. Contrasting last night's look with her indifferent manner toward him today, he wondered what had made her change so completely in the space of only a few hours. Unfortunately his own desire for her had not abated one whit. Just the sight of her lovely face, even if it was turned in profile, was enough to bring his pulse alive.

While Richard was thinking these thoughts, he unconsciously began to rub the sore muscles in his upper arm.

"Richard, is anything the matter?" Selina's tone was far more solicitous now.

It made him smile. He would appreciate a little sympathy at this moment. "Well," he said—quite temperately he thought—"that was rather difficult work you gave me this morning."

"Really?" Instead of contrition, all she seemed to feel was a detached interest. "I had not thought it so. But then"—she sighed quite audibly—"I have watched Romeo Fancible dig stumps a hundred times. And Romeo always makes everything look so easy."

She paused in her stirring to gaze into the distance with a wistful smile. "I suppose Romeo *is* much stronger than the average man. Quite strong, in fact. I'm sure you must have noticed his size. He is quite extraordinary."

As extraordinary as an ox in doublet and hose, Richard thought to himself before he realized what she was about. But then it came to him.

The graceless imp was trying to make him jealous!

Richard added this new insight to the suspicion he'd felt only a few moments before, and came up with the reason for her cool treatment. Selina was annoyed with him for withdrawing from their embrace last night. Her feelings had been wounded, so she was doing her best to attack his now. He had hurt her by using restraint, when he had done the only honorable thing a gentleman could do under the circumstances.

But regardless of his reasons, she was too inexperienced to interpret his qualms for what they were. She had reacted quite naturally, and she was handling her hurt the only way she knew how. With revenge.

Certain he understood her now, Richard smiled and agreed to her assessment of Romeo's strength with his teeth barely clenched. But Selina refused to let the subject of his morning's work drop.

"Perhaps," she suggested, brushing past Richard to set his place at the table, "you would rather be set to a different chore?"

"I would not object," Richard said, momentarily distracted by a whiff of her perfume, which again seemed new today. What was it? He didn't recognize the fragrance, though it did seem familiar. Whatever it was, it was damnably warm and enticing.

"I suppose you could cull seeds," she said in a condescending voice. Her back was toward him as she reached to place his silver. Her skirt swayed back and forth in front of him like a bird before a snake, focusing his eyes.

"I usually do that chore myself because it is so easy," she continued with her back still toward him. "It only consists of opening the fruit and scraping out the seeds, you know. It requires no strength at all, so I hate to waste Lucas's time with it. But if you think you truly cannot go on digging stumps—"

"No." Richard clamped his jaw down tightly. He refused to let himself be shamed, if that was what she wanted. He had rather take the punishment she had chosen for him instead. "I shall go on digging stumps."

"You're quite certain?" She turned and looked at him, anger and pain behind her eyes. "You're sure you haven't had enough?"

He squared his shoulders, then had to ignore the ache between them to respond. "Quite sure. I can think of nothing I would rather do."

Selina bit her lip. If she had expected any satisfaction from taunting him, she didn't appear to have felt it. Misery clouded her eyes.

"Thank you so much, Richard," she said, turning away.

The next day, Richard fared no better. Neither the next nor the next. And by the end of the week, he was cursing himself for a fool.

The only improvement in his days was that his painful muscles at last grew accustomed to so much use and stopped torturing him with every motion. Before reaching this point, he had laid down his tools many times with the intention of putting an end to his masquerade and leaving the Payleys to fend for themselves. But every time, some incident had occurred to put him off.

Whether, after searching for Selina, he found her performing a task nearly as difficult as the one he had been doing, or whether she managed to refer to Romeo in just that tone of voice to raise the hair on the back of his neck, something always made him return to his work.

From time to time, when Augustus was not occupied with his morning lessons with the vicar, he alleviated Richard's boredom by coming to work beside him. But this could not make up for the frustration Richard felt every time he spied Selina in the distance, looking more desirable, it seemed, every day. It could not keep him from thinking about her when he ought to be turning earth, or from remembering the sweetness of her scent the last time he had come within sniffing distance. Or from wondering just what it would feel like to kiss her and regretting the noble impulse that had stopped him from doing just that.

For it was one thing to think nobly about helping the girl with no reward and quite another to withstand the temptation of her every day.

A temptation Romeo had better resist, Richard vowed, clenching his jaw, if he wanted to live to see a riper age.

For Romeo had begun to visit Selina every morning, if, in fact, that had not been his practice before. It appeared that the sheep Selina used to graze and manure her orchards were Romeo's sheep. That circumstance, and his kinship with Nero, were more than sufficient excuse for his calls, for the sheep were purposely crowded in the orchard and could not flourish in the winter on Selina's grass alone. They had to be fed elsewhere as well, which meant that every day they had to be brought and retrieved.

Richard suspected that a servant with a dog could just as easily have done the fetching, yet Romeo persisted in coming for them himself. He never came without searching out Selina, nor did he choose a time when Augustus was at home.

Richard was surprised that Selina put up with such a transparent strategy, and was dismayed to see it working. As busy as she was, particularly when Richard had need of her attention, she could always spare a few minutes for Romeo.

Like today, when she had actually put down her gloves to join him at Nero's pen.

Busy in the sprig orchard when Romeo arrived,

Richard decided it was time to take a rest from his job. Telling Lucas to be sure not to disappear while he was gone, he laid down his shovel and strode purposefully to Nero's pen.

Romeo was leaning upon the fence, one enormous boot resting upon the bottom board, a long stick in his massive fist with which he was scratching Nero behind the ears. Selina had leaned her elbows on the top board as well, and her shawl stretched tightly across her shoulders. This gave Richard a chance to admire the way her back tapered gracefully to her slender waist.

The sound of Richard's boots on the gravel notified them of his approach. He saw Selina flash Romeo a smile so bright, it made the big oaf blush.

"Visiting your friend?" Richard said to Romeo, meaning the hog and not Selina.

Such ambiguity was lost upon Mr. Fancible. "Checking on pig," he muttered.

"Just as I thought." Richard nodded with an amiable smile. "Your devotion is admirable. I should think the pigs on your own farm must be quite as happy as larks if you give them but a tenth of the attention you give Nero."

With that he did manage to hit his mark, for Romeo squirmed as if he'd been caught in some naughty act.

Selina, who, to all appearances, had been ignoring Richard, smiled quite fondly at Romeo, swaying toward him.

Richard's fists clenched. His reaction surprised him for he was not used to having a temper, certainly not where a lady's attentions were involved. He had watched his own mistresses flirt with any number of men and remained entirely unmoved.

Thinking, perhaps, that that was the difference— Selina was *not* his paramour and was never likely to be, no matter how tempting she was—he tried to calm himself with a deep breath. Finding that it did not help much, he began to worry that performing so much physical labor might be turning him into an oaf as well. He had certainly lost all sense of what was due his dignity as a peer, and now he was reacting to this challenge like a bantam cock. He only hoped that the differences between himself and Romeo Fancible were still readily obvious.

But Selina, it appeared, did not welcome his intrusion. Reluctantly she turned from her swain to address Richard.

"Was there something you were needing, Mr. Lint?"

She called him that, he knew, for Romeo's sake. Yet it still made him bristle.

"Yes, I was wondering what delights you had planned for me for the rest of the day?" He paused. "Or for the evening?"

Richard knew he ought not to have added that last, but he had not missed the start in Romeo's eyes at his use of the word "delights," and he had not been able to prevent himself. His softer, more insinuating tone on the last phrase had been—he was ready to swear—by pure chance alone.

But he was gratified to see the effect his tone had had upon Selina. She had turned a most becoming shade of pink.

"I—will think of something else for today," she stammered, bringing her hands together. "But as for after dinner—"

She was going to say he would be dismissed as usual, but Richard would not let her say that in front of Romeo Fancible.

"After dinner . . . what?" He spoke in a warm, low voice and leaned to rest a hand on the post behind her, pinning her between his body and the fence.

Her eyes widened in shock. But there was something—

not at all like horror—behind them as well. Her breaths came in soft little gasps.

"After dinner. . . " She licked her lips.

"Yes . . . ?" he prompted, leaning nearer.

Out of the corner of his eye, Richard saw that Romeo's fist had curled into the shape of a rump roast. He felt a curious desire to fight him and surprisingly not the least bit of fear. Blood surged eagerly to his temples as Romeo took a step nearer.

His sudden motion to her right woke Selina, who darted one glance in Romeo's direction, before stepping quickly between them. She snapped out, "I cannot conceive of what you mean, Mr. Lint, when we never have set you to work after dark and you will very likely be in bed."

Her back was turned to Romeo. Richard could not resist one last attempt to discommode her. "Shall I?" he uttered so softly that no one but Selina could hear.

She gave another gasp. Her lips stayed parted, and Richard traced them with his eyes.

Her tongue ventured out to wet those lips again, and he was forced to clear his throat.

His limbs were humming. His pulse was roaring in his ears. This sparring with Selina had bolstered his spirits a thousandfold.

"Ur . . . Mistress Payley."

With a start, Selina seemed to remember the man behind her. She spun with an angry toss of her hair and took Romeo by the arm.

"I shall walk you to your horse, Mr. Fancible, and we shall discuss this season's crops on the way."

This conversational gambit nearly made Richard laugh out loud even though he had not missed her snub. He knew he had angered her, but he had excited her as well.

Greatly satisfied, he took himself back to the pasture

and finished his job before returning his tools to the barn. He was putting them up when Selina stormed in.

"Mr. Lint," she began with her hands on her hips.

"Richard—please," he begged her in his most congenial voice.

She stomped one foot. Richard did not think he had ever seen her appear more desirable than at that moment. Her rich brown eyes were flashing like logs aflame, her heaving breast had filled her bodice, and her cheeks had turned the deep red of cherry wine.

"I shall never"—she stomped on the word—"never address you as Richard again. How you could embarrass me so! And in front of Mr. Fancible, too! Why, my reputation will be ruined!"

Richard hid a smile and widened his eyes in a look of total innocence. "Selina, what can you mean?"

"You know what I mean. You implied"—her gaze slid to the floor—"you know very well what you implied."

"What—" Richard scratched his head, hoping to be at least a bit convincing. "What did I imply?"

She darted an angry glance his way. "You know. That you and I—that we—" With a flurry of her fingers, she gave it up. "I cannot imagine what possessed you to act in that extraordinary fashion."

"That we . . . ?" Richard hoped to prompt the rest from her, at which point he would be happy to oblige.

But Selina was far too embarrassed for that. He had disturbed her far more than he had intended, and his pretense of innocence had done much worse. She was truly angry now and close to tears.

Regret engulfed him. Richard abandoned his pose and took a step toward her. He wished he could fold her in his arms, but knew now was not the time. "I am sincerely sorry if I've said something to discomfit you in front of your neighbor. If I can make it up to you, I will be happy to oblige."

She surprised him by wailing miserably, "I thought that Romeo was going to hit you. Which would have been your own fault! But you should not go around provoking men twice your size with no regard for the consequences."

"Twice my size?" Richard couldn't restrain a protest. "I think you exaggerate. I know that Romeo is as big and as clumsy as a barn, but I'm not precisely the puny fellow you paint me. I've been known to deck more than one six-foot man before."

"And so you would go brawling about my barnyard? And teasing Romeo, who has not done anything to deserve such inconsiderate treatment?"

Richard felt a seed of remorse entering his heart. It had been petty of him to use his brain against one no better than a cow's. "If what I said was unkind or unfair, you have my apology."

"It is Romeo's apology you should seek. Do I need to remind you in what position he stands to me?"

Richard's head shot up. Selina met his eye, then looked away.

All of a sudden he was aware of the silence in the barn, the rustle of the hay as he shifted his feet, the sound of her uneven breathing.

His hackles were on the rise. "No," he said, suppressing them. "You have no need to remind me."

"Good." She bobbed her head, her eyes still averted. "Then, no more on the subject need be said. You will excuse me, please."

With that, and much to his dismay, she hurriedly left the barn, giving her hair a brisk flick over her shoulder.

Richard turned quickly back to his tools, muttering a curse under his breath. He had not meant to injure her so. All he had wanted—

All he had wanted was to shake her from the indifference she had been showing him. It was one thing to withdraw from an ill-advised kiss. Quite another to treat him as if he didn't exist. But Selina seemed determined to punish him for his restraint.

He had laid his hands upon her shoulders and, despite the warm feel of her under his palms, had tried his best not to seduce her. And he had succeeded, too, though his success had cost him dearly that night. In spite of the wintry air, he had been forced to indulge in a cold-water wash.

It was the closest he had ever come to kissing a woman and not done so. And *this* was what he had earned.

A heavy sigh came from somewhere behind him. Richard turned to see Lucas at the door of the barn, leaning on a shovel.

"Women," the old man said, shaking his head.

"I beg your pardon?" Richard raised an offended brow. "Were you eavesdropping?"

"Who me?" Lucas shook his head rapidly before a look of low cunning swept his face. "No . . . wouldn't do that," he said.

"Wouldn't you." Richard said this in a tone that stopped just short of calling Lucas an out-and-out liar. "Then, what, pray, is the reason for such a comment?"

Lucas scratched the back of his head, undoubtedly freeing a few pair of lice. Since Selina had recently stood in just that spot, Richard felt more than his usual repugnance upon seeing present company. But it appeared that Lucas had come to chat, probably to avoid his next duty. For once, Richard lacked the strength of will to see that he kept to his work.

"Only said something," Lucas ventured, casting an eye Richard's way, " 'cause I've got a kind o' way with women."

"You?" The notion was preposterous. "You are something of an expert, are you?"

"Yessir." Lucas hefted one shoulder as if the burdens for one of his talents had been great. "Knows 'un front'ards and back'ards, so to speak."

I'll bet you do, you rascal. Thinking this to himself, Richard hoped he would not be treated to a chronicle of Lucas's more lurid escapades, when what he needed was a little peace and quiet to sort out his thoughts. "That still doesn't excuse the comment you made when you came in."

Lucas eyed him from under his brows. Seeing nothing in Richard's present manner to alarm him, he volunteered, "Mistress Payley looked to be in a bit of a huff." His stare probed Richard in a way that would have made him squirm if it had come from anyone else. "Thought maybe you'd scared her, like."

"Your mistress has nothing to fear from me, and she knows it. You needn't concern yourself."

Richard turned back to his shovel. He hoped that Lucas would go away, but instead the old rascal settled himself down in a pile of hay for a comfortable snooze.

After a few minutes, he spoke from beneath his disreputable hat. "Yessir, I guess women are like horses."

Richard's patience wore thin. He could not allow Lucas to discuss Selina in any terms, much less such disrespectful ones. "I am sure," he said in a tone that brooked no argument, "that you would never include Miss Payley in your idle chatter."

"Oh, no." The shake Lucas gave his head did not convince Richard, but he let it pass. "Not Mistress Payley. Not in particular. But, when ye get right down to it, I guess they're all alike."

Richard supposed that for someone like Lucas—a *homo vulgaris* if ever there was one—this gross simplification might be true. Lucas would not have the delicacy of mind to perceive even the most obvious differences between women, much less the good taste to recognize his own mistress's superiority. The thought that such a disreputable example of humanity should consider himself an expert upon its better half made Richard almost sick.

"So you've had a great experience of women," Richard said, shaking his head at the absurdity.

"Yessir. More than ye might think."

That would be for certain. "And what has this vast experience taught you?"

Lucas did not trouble to raise himself to a sitting position as he removed the hat from his eyes. "Seems to me, ye've got to think like one of 'un to get what ye want."

"Yes?" Richard truly was amused now—enough to listen. "And you can do this, can you?"

Still lying down, Lucas managed a shrug that was half-cocky, half-modest. "S'pose I can at that."

"So tell me, Lucas, how do women think?"

A pained expression came over his face. "Can't tell ye everything. T'all depends, ye see, on what's a-doing."

"On what is going on between you and your lady friend? Is that what you mean?"

"That's so." Lucas nodded the way a teacher might nod to an apt pupil. "That would be the way of it."

Richard was on the point of setting forth a hypothetical situation for Lucas to analyze, one that bore an astonishing resemblance to his own dilemma with Selina, when he took himself up short.

What on God's earth was he doing?

Turning back to his tools, Richard felt a wave of disgust roll over him. How had he managed to get himself into this ridiculous situation? Here he was, discussing his most intimate concerns with a man who smelled like a manure pile. It was simply one more piece of evidence that working as a common laborer on a farm was making him lose his veneer of civilization. Why, next he would be discussing slops with Nero!

If he had hoped by turning his back to put an end to Lucas's discourse, he was destined for disappointment. The lazy braggart was determined to pontificate upon women as he did upon everything else, and it was clear that he would not leave Richard alone until he'd made his point. Richard would not, however, be drawn into any conversation with Lucas in which Selina might play the slightest part.

As Lucas rattled on behind him, likening girls to troublesome fillies in a most unoriginal way, Richard pondered his current predicament. The shame he'd felt on causing Selina distress had not yet lost its sting. Neither had the sickening feeling that had washed over him when she had reminded him of her inevitable relationship to Romeo. It had helped not one whit that he had suspected her of trying to arouse his jealousy.

With his experience of women—all far more sophisticated than she—Richard ought to have been able to ignore Selina's simple attempts to make him jealous.

That he had not was what confused him. Selina's tactics—the way she so pointedly turned her back on him, the way she fawned over Romeo whenever Richard was near—were rudimentary at best. They were the sort of trick a schoolgirl might get up to, far simpler than what might be devised by an experienced London flirt. But then, Selina lacked the experience of a common London flirt.

Any oaf could see through her tactics, perhaps better even than she. And if he could see through them so easily, why were they so damned effective? Why did the hair on the scruff of his neck rise whenever she so much as mentioned Romeo Fancible?

"O' course"—Lucas's voice floated up behind him, breaking into his thoughts—"one thing ye do notice about women is that they're a bit like cows."

"Like cows! Why, you old goat!"

Richard spun angrily and took a step toward him, but Lucas remained unruffled, his hat still resting over his eyes.

"Not so's yer thinking," he said slowly. He seemed in no particular hurry to amend his insult. "I mean, it's their tails."

Richard closed his eyes in an effort to control his temper. "You think that improves upon your offensive remark?"

"It's the way they toss it—their hair, ye know. Like a cow tosses her tail when she see her bull a-coming."

Neatly flummoxed, Richard was about to give up in disgust when a memory came to him. Selina *had* tossed her hair his way when she had left the barn.

Richard recognized many a flirtatious movement practiced by ladies of the ton, but none of them wore their hair down their backs like Selina. It would be practically impossible, and certainly ill-advised, to try to toss a *coiffure à la greque* over one's shoulder.

Though Richard hated to admit it, Lucas had hit upon a point Richard had not considered. Selina's attempts to punish him and to make him jealous might certainly be intended to goad him into action. A flick of the tail, as it were, in his direction. She had wanted him to kiss her, he had thought at the time. Instead of being grateful to him for reining himself in, she had resented the blow to her amour propre.

He knew that she was proud. In his attempts to circumnavigate that pride, he might have done the one unforgivable thing: to lead her to commit herself with her eyes, then to beat a retreat. He tried to imagine how she would have felt and had no difficulty, for it was probably the way he felt every time she rubbed in the fact that she was contemplating marriage with a man so far beneath her.

Richard still thought he had done the honorable thing under these strange circumstances, but that did not mean he could not offer her a balm to her pride. It would be the easiest thing in the world to make Selina realize how desirable he found her, as easy as concealing his admiration had been difficult.

Richard could almost smile now at her determination to make him suffer, for she certainly had. His Selina was no shrinking violet.

Remembering that Lucas was nearby, Richard shook himself out of his contemplation. The scoundrel probably knew what he'd been talking about all along, but he would never dare be direct. Not if it meant losing his post.

Convinced the most dignified exit would be to leave with no further words, Richard took himself off at once, not entirely sorry that he had paused long enough to listen. If Selina needed someone to show her how desirable she was, then Richard considered himself to be amply qualified.

Chapter Nine

"Are you angry with Richard?" Augustus's troubled voice pierced Selina's reverie.

They were sitting near the hearth after supper, Selina with a basket of needlework on her lap, Augustus with a book held up to the dim firelight. Selina had been thinking of Richard, her needle paused in midair. Trying not to show how much her brother's question had startled her, she hastily took up her mending and applied herself to it again.

"No, of course I'm not angry with him," she said as evenly as she could. "What made you ask?"

Augustus shrugged, and a frown of boyish perplexity came over his face. Glancing at the book he had put down, Selina saw that he had not made much progress on his Latin, scarcely more than she had made on her stitching.

In typical Augustus fashion, however, he did not answer her at once, but withheld his response until he had given the matter proper consideration. When he did, his words were enough to make her flush.

"You never speak to Richard kindly. You give him the most unpleasant chores to do. And you never smile at him any more."

Selina had not felt like smiling for many days, and just now, she felt most unreasonably like crying, but she had never stopped to think what effect her mood would have upon her brother. She had supposed, if she had thought about it at all, that his youth would protect him from noticing the troubles of his elders, but she saw she had underestimated Augustus's perspicacity.

"You needn't worry," she told him gently. "I do like Mr. Lint, and I shall be grateful to him, too, if his cousin turns up the evidence we are seeking."

"Then, why do you treat Richard worse than you treat Lucas?"

"I do not!"

"Yes, you do. You would never give Lucas so much work that he nearly missed dinner, or expect him to plant new trees by himself."

"That is because Lucas requires a great deal of supervision, while Rich"—she caught herself before speaking his name—"while *Mr. Lint* seems perfectly able to care for himself."

"And you called him Richard before, but now you call him Mr. Lint."

Selina could say nothing in rebuttal. Unfortunately Augustus had been present when she had made that rash decision, which had done nothing but bring an unwarranted degree of familiarity into her dealings with Richard. A familiarity on her part only, it seemed, which had gone no further on his, no matter what her dreams upon the subject had been. No matter what silliness her mind had concocted or her foolish heart had allowed.

But it would not do to let Augustus know the extent of her confusion and despair.

"I have decided to call him Mr. Lint," she said, "to observe the proprieties. You are only a boy, Augustus. You do not know how society works, but Mr. Lint's continuation at the Grange could appear to be something quite other than it is."

"How do you know that it isn't?" Augustus floored her by asking.

The blood drained from her cheeks, then flooded them. "How do I know it isn't what?" Her question came out in a whisper.

"How do you know why he's staying?"

"I—presume his motives are what he has stated them to be," Selina said, flustered. "It would be most improper of me to presume anything else."

"You mean, what he said about learning to tend an orchard?"

"Of course."

"Oh, fiddle!" Augustus's face registered disgust. "Any gentleman with Richard's intelligence could learn everything he needed to know about orchards in one day!"

"In . . . one day?"

He nodded. "He has his own land; he said so himself. So he already would know how to drain it and get it ready for planting. All he would need would be a bit more information about fruit trees. When to plant and harvest them . . . how and when to prune . . . which variety to grow in his own county . . . a handful of facts."

"Then . . ." Something about Augustus's words had set a bell to ringing deep inside Selina. "Then, what you are saying is, Richard must have some other reason for staying at the Grange?"

Augustus nodded again. In his eyes a question lurked, almost as if he did not know whether to ask. "Yes, and I thought you might know what his reason was."

"No"—Selina shook her head vehemently—"No, I have not the slightest idea."

In fact, the notion that Richard might have some ulterior motive for staying at the Grange had never occurred to her. These past few days, she had been so wrapped up in her own misery, she had hardly been able to think logically. And, she realized both suddenly and painfully, from the moment he had first appeared, she had ignored any question her brain might have posed.

Such as, who was Richard? Was he a farmer or someone more important? How big was his estate? Where *did* he come from—was his land in Kent or as far away as Yorkshire? Was it somewhere that cherry trees could even grow? She had no idea. And, most importantly, she had never learned how he had found the Grange in the first place.

Selina had purposely refused to ask any questions of the sort for fear of chasing him off. First, perhaps, because she had needed his business so desperately. But now, oh, now she admitted, because she did not wish him to go. She had refused to listen to the voice inside her because she had wanted him to stay. She had not wanted to believe he had another life away from her and the Grange.

While she was dismally acknowledging these motives, Augustus stayed silent, but then he spoke.

"Well, I *do* like Richard."

"You do?" Selina could not keep a pathetic plea from creeping into her voice. "Why?"

Augustus gave a jerk to his head to flick the hair out of his eyes. Her brother, Selina noticed guiltily, had been woefully neglected and was in desperate need of a haircut.

"Oh, I don't know," Augustus mused. "I guess because he tackles the work as if it were play. I don't mean that he doesn't do a good job, because he does. It's more as if he knows there are more important things than mucking out a barn, but he's content to do it for now.

"And he discusses my lessons with me as if I were more than just a boy. I can't help liking that. I mean—" Augustus stared down at his boots. He seemed to find them riveting all of a sudden. "Romeo could never discuss my schoolwork with me. He hasn't read since he was in school, if he ever did."

"Why did you bring up Romeo?" Selina asked uncomfortably.

"Well . . ." Augustus gulped, and the hint of rose beneath his skin surprised her. "I thought that maybe the reason Richard was staying might have something to do with you"—his words tumbled faster—"I know he likes you, because he's always looking at you the way Rufus Croft looks at the blacksmith's daughter—the one who giggles, you know. And if that was it, then I wanted you to know which one I liked best."

"Which—" Selina felt her pulse picking up again. "Which one you liked best?"

She tried to make her question sound more casual than it was. If Augustus had noticed so much—and she could almost kick herself for not being a tenth as aware as he—then, perhaps he had remarked something about Richard's intentions that she herself had failed to note. And, if so, she absolutely must hear it.

But Augustus could not be more specific. When prodded, he responded that it seemed Richard spent a great deal of time staring after her. It seemed to Augustus, too, that Richard's interest in trees was spurious at best. His innate courtesy kept him focused on Augustus's words whenever the boy tried to explain some simple principle of orcharding, but his mind always seemed to be half somewhere else.

And Augustus had begun to suspect that somewhere was wherever his sister happened to be.

As grateful as she was to her brother for opening her eyes, and as touched by his concern, Selina soon cut off this discussion. She could not let herself believe that Richard had stayed at the Grange to be near her—not when he had turned down the opportunity to kiss her she had so blatantly offered him. At least she had supposed it was blatant enough, though knowing so little about Richard and nothing at all about kissing, perhaps she had mistakenly thought it so.

Perhaps Richard would need more encouragement than she had given him. She was, after all, a lady and mistress of her own establishment. Perhaps he had been too shy, too intimidated by her status, to be forward.

Or perhaps—this frightening thought made her fight to suppress it—perhaps he had some other motive in mind, which had nothing at all to do with her. But Selina could not speculate upon that without the ground opening to swallow her heart whole. . . .

Unable to stand her quandary a moment longer, Selina stood abruptly, grabbed up a pair of shears, and set about the task of trimming Augustus's shaggy locks.

The next day, she was both surprised and disarmed when Richard paid her a compliment upon her hair. She had greeted him with a trifle more cordiality this morning. A very . . . nervous cordiality. Sooner or later, she knew, she would have to discover why he had chosen to stay and when he would be leaving. She thought it must have been the change in her tone that had drawn the comment from him, for he had smiled at her at once and said, "The morning sun makes your hair shine like the finest mahogany."

Now, Selina had taken great pains with her hair that morning, brushing it briskly for more than two hundred strokes and only giving up when she could not lift the brush any longer. But Richard could not be aware of that, could he?

His remark left her stammering, so the order she gave him came out with much less sting than she had been using of late.

"If you would like, you could help me in the barn this morning."

His reply, "It is always a pleasure to work beside you," nearly took her breath away.

Selina's knees felt unsteady as she led the way into the barn. Richard reached past her and lifted open the heavy, sagging door.

"You ought to let me get someone out to repair this for you," he said, heaving it back into place.

"Lucas can do it," Selina said in the automatical way she always used to cope with such issues.

"Ah, Lucas." Richard's comment was accompanied by a teasing grin. "And when do you think he might get to this particular task?"

Selina knew she ought to take offense, but when Richard smiled at her in that way, she could not. She had missed his smiles. "I shall make a note on his calendar for tomorrow, and his engagement secretary will remind him."

She could see how surprised he was by her good humor. He stared at her out of dark blue eyes that seemed to deepen in intensity. The sweet smell of hay surrounded them, the warmth of the barn.

Selina returned his stare, wishing she knew how to provoke a man into declaring himself. She could not be certain Richard was timid. He did not seem so, not in the way that Romeo was, but then—What other consideration could restrain a man? Richard's compliments had been uttered without a trace of nervousness. Why, then, did he refuse to kiss her?

Selina felt a desperate need to know once and for all.

Richard broke their locked gazes before she did and cleared his throat. Flustered by her lack of success, Selina felt her temper start to rise.

But she would not let it get the best of her today. *She would not!*

"What would you have me do in here?" Richard asked after a pause.

"You can help me pitch hay for Caesar and Clarissa."

He raised his brow and grinned. "After all I have been doing, this sounds positively like a holiday."

Selina felt a blush stealing its way up her neck, which would surely give her away if he saw it. Her leniency, if he could only see, was more in the nature of an invitation.

She asked Richard to fetch the pitchforks and join her up in the loft. Grasping her skirt in one hand, she climbed the rickety ladder to be ready to receive the tools when he passed them up.

Richard did so, then scaled the ladder in three giant steps, making the loft sag with each one. Alarmed by the ominous way it dipped, Selina hoped fleetingly that the ancient structure could hold both their weights, but its movement ceased once Richard stood at the top.

The barn ceiling was too low for them to stand perfectly erect. It had not been built for people their size. Bent at the waist, Selina began to fear she had chosen a poor spot to flirt. Feeling awkward, she speared hay and tossed it down.

Mindful of her prongs, Richard followed suit, choosing a spot behind her.

Selina bent and scooped five times before she noticed that Richard had done nothing. Glancing back, she was annoyed to find him leaning on his pitchfork, one arm crossed on top of the other, watching her work with a curiously intent stare.

"Richard?" she prodded him.

With a start he came to attention, and as their eyes met, a smile spread slowly across his features. "Pardon?" he said.

"I believe you were gathering wool." She tried to

sound disapproving, though his smile had set her pulse to beating wildly.

"Not at all," he said with that still lazy smile. "Simply appreciating the view."

A slow comprehension filled her, like water seeping into a sponge. But before she could react, down below Caesar gave out a great bellow, which shook the rafters. Feeling the loft rattle beneath her, Selina caught at an ancient support. Her startled expression made Richard laugh, which angered and thrilled her all at once.

"Why, you!"

She grabbed her pitchfork and flung a load of hay in his face, a trick she'd played on Augustus countless times to stem his impudence.

Richard threw up a hand to protect himself, but not before a shower of straw rained down upon his head and shoulders.

Her sudden giggle raised a light in his eyes. "I shall have to take my revenge."

Caught in that light, Selina had not felt so much fright since she had last searched under her bed for a hobgoblin. "You wouldn't dare."

"Wouldn't I, though?"

The gleam in Richard's eye set her pulse to thumping. Half-terrified, she launched another clump his way, mantling his head.

He made a fake lunge for her.

A hysterical shriek escaped her before she clapped a hand over her mouth. The spark in Richard's eyes had turned to thunder.

Selina stood paralyzed while he removed his tight-fitting jacket and stock, and shook out his hair. Bits of hay and errant weeds had stuck throughout his short, dark locks.

"You, my girl," he said in a deep, villainous whisper, "are in for a great deal of trouble."

Selina dropped her pitchfork, meaning to make a dash for the ladder, but Richard's scoopful of straw landed squarely in her face. It smothered her eyes and lungs, and she coughed, sputtering.

A bigger shower sprinkled her head, raining hay into her mouth.

"Th-thtop!" she pleaded as she laughed, trying to pull the pieces from her tongue. A slither of hay slid inside the neck of her gown, and she groaned at the tickle between her breasts. "Pleathe, thtop."

"I'll *th-thtop*," Richard teased, "if you swear a pax."

"Pax. Pax," she declared, not meaning one word of it. Selina bent as if to shake the hay from her hair, but snatched up her weapon instead.

She barely saw Richard's attack. He had her pitchfork in one hand, his arm about her waist before she could breathe.

"I knew I shouldn't trust you," he growled near her ear. "Not with a temper as hot as yours."

"I wasn't angry," Selina said, panting and laughing.

"No?" His smile was only inches from her lips. "Now, that would be a change."

Abruptly Selina became aware that his other arm had encircled her, too. Richard had dropped the pitchfork, but he had not released her.

"Don't you trust me now?" she asked breathlessly. Her gaze moved to the place where his shirt gaped open, then back to his eyes.

Exultantly she recognized in them the same excitement she felt.

"Should I let you go?"

His meaning was unclear, his face poised on a slant with her own. She could feel his breath against her lips.

Still uncertain, Selina paused before giving a rash shake to her head.

He moaned. "Oh, give it up, Richard," he said under his breath. "She's much too lovely to let go."

He joined his lips with hers, fiercely at first, but then they softened. Selina was floating, floating in his arms while the hay swirled about them. Then, with a start, she realized that she truly was suspended, for he had swooped her up off the floor.

He laid her down in a soft stack of hay, then came to rest beside her, one leg crossed with hers.

"Selina . . ." he breathed her name like some sort of prayer. "Selina, you've been so hard to resist."

Joy shot through her on a trembling wave, cresting near her lips. She wanted to cry out with the pleasure his hands were working.

He stroked her hair, fanning it out on the hay with his fingers, then brushed her cheeks and nose and forehead with kisses. Selina gave a blissful sigh.

The sound made him pause, and he frowned.

"Selina, there is something you ought to know."

Do not say anything that will make you stop.

He seemed to read the plea in her eyes, for he gave up talking and kissed her again, a slow, sweet kiss, which she hoped would never end. She wrapped her arms about his neck.

The prickle of hay broke through her dreaminess and made her squirm against him.

"Wait, love," Richard said in a husky moan. "You had better stop wriggling, or I shall not be able to answer for my actions."

Afraid that he had mistaken her movement for wantonness, Selina protested shyly, "It's the hay. It's making me itch."

"Oh." He chuckled and looked down at her dress. His laughter ceased. "Then, let me remove it for you."

Something in his tone sent a tremor rocking through

her. But she held still for him. His movements were chaste, cautious, and delicate as one by one he lightly plucked the hay from the front of her garment. His fingers never lingered in any spot for too long, but Selina still felt their tender caress. With his every light touch—on her collar, her waist, her breast—she felt anticipation rising. By the time he had removed all of the hay, she was trembling from head to toe.

Some mysterious force she could not deny pulled her to a sitting position. She lifted her hair to expose her neck. "There are more here," she said, throwing the heavy fall to one side.

Richard took a place behind her. She could both hear and feel him, though he was hidden from her eyes. A gentle brush of his fingertips raised gooseflesh on her neck, and she shivered with a pleasurable fright. Then, as his lips followed their path, her head fell back and she closed her eyes.

"Selina." Her whispered name sounded somewhere near her ear. "Selina, you must promise me one important thing."

"What?" She could barely speak for the thrills of delight chasing one another down her spine.

"You must promise me that you will not"—he punctuated each word with a soft kiss upon her neck—"that you will never—marry—Mr. Romeo—Fancible."

A wave of excitement rolled through her, the first real surge of confidence she had ever felt. It melted her inside, bringing tears to her eyes. Without a moment's hesitation, she promised with a tremor in her voice, "Very well, I shall not." She had far rather give herself to Richard.

"Good girl." With those words Richard turned her by the shoulders until she faced him again. His own breathing was shallow and quick. His lips were parted.

Focusing on those lips, Selina sank back into the straw. His body covered hers.

The loft gave a dip.

They paused. But, when nothing happened, they ignored the warning in favor of something far more exciting. The air around them seemed to be filled with a force, so magical that nothing else could possibly matter. Adrift in its fevered atmosphere, Selina shuttered her eyes as Richard's body weighted hers down.

Another dip, with a loud creaking of timbers.

Selina's eyes shot open. As the floor lurched beneath them, Richard gathered her in his arms. He rolled her over on her side as the loft collapsed.

Startled and screaming, Selina hit the floor of the stall below, felt the weight of Richard's body as it crashed against hers. Though her teeth had been rattled by the crash, the hay had broken their fall. A cloud of dust swirled around them, making her cough, but when the air cleared, she saw Richard's worried face.

He brought her closer, if such a thing were even possible. "Selina, are you hurt?"

Carefully—suspicious of her lack of bruises—she tested each limb, then her back and her head. Widening her eyes, she gave her head a little shake.

"No, I don't think so," she whispered. "But my barn surely is."

Richard's lips quivered. Selina felt a bubble of joy just waiting to burst. With a flood of relief, they both gave in to laughter. Richard toppled on his back, rolling her over on top of him.

Selina found herself propped on her elbows, lying upon Richard's chest. He did not seem to be uncomfortably crushed.

"Selina Payley, you are the woman of my dreams."

Selina looked down at his gleaming eyes, and her heart nearly burst at what she saw.

Shyly now, still uncertain as to how to proceed, she let her instincts guide her. She raised a hand to touch his cheek. He closed his eyes as if in pain.

"Am I too heavy for you?" Selina struggled to remove herself, but his arms lashed more tightly around her.

"Heavy? No. Tempting? Yes."

When he opened his eyes again, she could not deny the fire she saw inside them. Frightened, but reassured at the same time, she could only squeak.

"Tempting? Me?"

In answer Richard rolled her off again, his body melding with hers. She felt his fingers at her bodice, felt them loosening it.

With a low moan of pleasure she could not conceal, Selina arched in his arms.

Someone loudly cleared his throat, and she froze.

"Rusticating, cuz?" a voice said.

At the sound of the weary drawl, Richard went rigid against her. His brows snapped together.

"Well, deary me," the voice said. "And here I was, thinking you had been waylaid by thugs and held to hostage, when all the time you was playing at husbandry with the dairymaid."

Rage, cold rage, stared out from Richard's eyes. But the stranger's remarks had slapped Selina in the face. She could feel her cheeks burning. She covered them both with her hands as Richard pried himself off her.

She was fumbling with her bodice, which had only been partially disturbed, when Richard reached down to help her up. He would not let her turn away, but made her stand close beside him as he greeted the newcomer.

Selina hung her head so as not to reveal her face. Hay and rotted wood filled her vision. Her pulse hammered in her ears. She shook her head to clear the sound, but shame kept it beating at a fever pitch, which dimmed the men's voices.

"Wilfrid." Richard's tone was enough to make anyone start. "You will apologize at once to Miss Payley."

He was trembling. Out of the corner of her eye, Selina could see his features quivering, whether from unanswered lust or the purest rage, she could not tell. But her own knees had nearly lost the strength to hold her up.

"*Miss* Payley? Oh, my heedless tongue! But, my dear, you must forgive me!"

Sensing the stranger's insincerity, Selina slowly raised her gaze to take him in, and received a shock.

The most frivolous dandy she had ever beheld stood just inside the door to her barn, bewigged, rouged, and patched, in the finest silk hosiery, pink inexpressibles, a polka dot waistcoat and lavender frock coat. He took one look at her flushed face and smirked, before raising a fan to hide his lips.

"My dear, you have my deepest, most profound apology. But what was one to think when my dear cousin Linton went disappearing? Then, when I posted down in breathless horror of finding him dead, I was surprised, nay shocked, to discover him rolling about in a crumbling barn. I heard the crash, you know, as I was walking about trying to knock somebody up at the house—which, by the way, appears to be quite unattended. Your servants, ma'am, should be reprimanded for leaving it so open to theft. But where was I—" He tapped his fan on his chin.

"Oh, yes," he continued, "I heard this quite alarming crash coming from the barn, and naturally ran to investigate. Richard"—the dandy made this aside in a lowered voice—"I hope this can be put down as proof of my fond attachment to you, for I scarcely heeded my own safety in doing so. Nevertheless, you can imagine my relief at finding not only that there were no ruffians inside, but that you were indeed alive and in such *obvious* good health—"

The dandy raked them both with hooded eyes, not missing a detail of their dishevelment: their loosened clothes; the remnants of their hay fight; Richard's heightened color; and Selina's tattered gown. "*That*, I hope, at least will excuse my very poor manners."

Selina's senses were still dulled by the throbbing in her ears, but his words soon pierced her consciousness. She jerked her chin into the air. She would not be insulted by a dandy. No matter that his clothes were so much finer than hers. No matter who he was.

Richard's cousin.

Richard's voice cut across this realization. "Wilfrid, what are you doing here?"

Richard's anger had only slightly softened. She could hear it in the biting tone of his voice.

This note, one she had never heard in it before, almost made him a stranger to her, too.

Linton. This Wilfrid person had called him Linton.

"Richard—" Selina drew herself up even though her recognition of that name made her want to sink beneath the earth. She hoped the tremor in her heart did not reach her voice. "Who is this gentleman, please?"

He made a move toward her as if to take her hand, but she hastily stepped away.

Stunned by her gesture, Richard hesitated, then bowed. "Miss Payley, may I present a distant cousin of mine, Sir Wilfrid Bart?"

Sir Wilfrid Bart, she heard, and her world shattered. His rank, his dress, his insufferable smugness proclaimed him to be far above her own station.

But the dandy was making her a leg, and she had to keep her shock from showing.

"Miss Payley." The insinuation in his voice slid over her like oil. "Any *friend* of my dear cousin Linton's is a friend of mine."

The repetition of Richard's true name made her want to flinch, but Selina held her head stiffly.

"And you, sir," she said to Richard in a frosty tone, "would be the Earl of Linton?"

She prayed that he would deny it, that she could believe him if he did.

But all Richard did was to stare back at her with a frown in his eyes. He made her a bow, far deeper than the one his cousin had made.

"At your service, my dear."

Chapter Ten

*R*ichard had seen the soft glow vanish from Selina's eyes. Her accusing stare had struck like a blow to his abdomen, so he did not see the benefit of his cousin's next remark.

"Oh, dear," Wilfrid said in politely distressed tones. "I fear I have appeared at a most awkward time."

Much worse than awkward, Richard thought. Wilfrid could not have chosen a more damaging moment if he had maliciously set out to do so; but, angry as he was at the interruption, Richard could not accuse his cousin of that.

He also could not explain himself to Selina with Wilfrid listening, yet he knew he had to do something to remove the hurt he had inflicted upon her as soon as possible.

He was on the point of asking Wilfrid to excuse them both, when Selina stepped into the breach.

"Not at all," she said with her beautiful chin in the air. "It appears that you have come at a most *propitious* time."

Richard winced. She clearly thought that Wilfrid had saved her from a fate worse than death.

"May I presume," she continued icily, "that you are the cousin—" She faltered, then recovered herself. "The cousin Lord Linton has spoken of? The gentleman who was to search the Cuckfield registers for proof of my ancestor's marriage?"

A glimmer of comprehension lit Wilfrid's eyes. He inclined his head. When he spoke, his voice was tinged with the utmost regret.

"I am indeed Linton's messenger. But alas, I can only bring you news that I fear must distress you. I am afraid there is no evidence of such a marriage left in Cuckfield."

Richard felt a sinking inside him, a surprisingly keen disappointment. The evidence that would have allowed him to throw his mantle over the Payleys had not materialized. He had not realized until that precise moment just how strongly he had wanted it to exist. And if he felt it, he knew that Selina was suffering far worse.

Ignoring Wilfrid, Richard reached out a hand to touch her shoulder. But she suddenly whirled to face him with such fury in her eyes, he felt like stepping back.

"You may reserve your condolences, *sir*, for someone who needs them. I believe I understand quite perfectly why your cousin discovered no proof of our kinship."

Feeling as if a ball of shot had just ripped him in the chest, Richard could only stare after her as she turned next to Wilfrid. "I must commend you, Sir Wilfrid, for such *assiduous* devotion to your cousin's interest."

With that last accusation, only thinly veiled, Selina turned with a stiff motion and hurried from the barn, leaving an empty silence in her wake.

Richard, who had recoiled from her implications, felt as if his blood had begun to churn. Anger at her unjust assumptions warred with the guilt he harbored for knowingly deceiving her as to his true identity. He knew his behavior, no matter how well-intentioned he had thought it, had been underhanded and reprehensible. He had done his best to become intimately acquainted with two persons without allowing them to know his name. He had assumed upon their ignorance to linger among them for his own ends, a motive he had been reluctant to admit to himself, but which was painfully obvious to him now.

He had stayed with the hope of bringing Selina to his bed.

Even now the frustration of that wish had left him trembling, so much so that he was at pains to distinguish how much of his reaction was due to unfulfilled lust and how much to anger. And to have Wilfrid, of all people, witness his just deserts . . .

Wilfrid's voice cut in. "I say, dear boy, I hope you will forgive my inopportune interruption. If I had had any notion of what might be going on in this dilapidated structure, I would never have—"

"Just why did you come, Wilfrid?" Richard was in no mood to hear his cousin's wanderings.

"But, Richard," Wilfrid said plaintively, "I thought I had explained it all most clearly. You see, when your note came to me, my suspicions were at once aroused by your failure to frank it. I was most concerned, nay grievously so. It quite truly appeared as if someone might have tampered with the letter. Nevertheless, knowing you to be disgustingly fit and strong, I supposed you able to take perfect care of yourself. I obeyed your summons to the letter and faithfully searched all the miserable little churches and chapels for miles about Cuckfield. And, at this point, cuz, I absolutely must protest the futility of such a mission. If there is one crumbling, drafty, mildewing edifice in Cuckfield, there must be a thousand in the surrounding few miles. I hope you do not plan to have me investigate any further such claims, for if you do, I am afraid I shall take my death of cold."

Richard felt like striking the peevish expression from his cousin's face, but he knew he was wrong to feel that way. He could not blame Wilfrid for his own mistakes. If he had truly wished to do Selina a service, he ought to have gone himself.

"That does not explain why you came here instead of sending word as I had expressly asked."

"Dear boy"—Wilfrid seemed sincerely hurt by his displeasure— "if you plan to take the habit of disappearing without one word of explanation either to your servants or to your relatives, simply inform me now, and I shall wash my hands of you. But what was one to think when you appeared to vanish off the face of the earth without a trace? Should I have meekly handed over a ransom to the first person so bold as to demand one, or should I—as I was persuaded you would wish me to do—show the courage you so often accuse me of lacking and come in search?"

Richard was about to protest the nonsense in Wilfrid's logic, but his cousin's expression changed.

"And," Wilfrid continued, his gaze burrowing deeply into Richard's conscience, "I have to confess no small degree of shock at finding you engaged in activities that quite frankly have the appearance of a clandestine affair. I very much fear, both from what I was told at the inn you directed me to, and from the umbrage that unhappy young lady has just taken, that she had not been fully apprised of your identity."

Wilfrid's last words had been uttered in a tone of mild reproof. To be the object of his cousin's disapproval on top of his other indignities was more than Richard could bear. He quite saw that this whole ghastly, disturbing episode had been his fault from beginning to end, and he would be immensely fortunate if Selina ever consented to forgive him.

By the look on her face as she had left the barn, Richard judged it would be quite some time, if ever, before that happy event could ever take place.

He could not help thinking, however, that if Wilfrid had turned up the evidence she was seeking, she would feel more in charity with him now. As it was, she clearly believed him to have conducted a false search in order to prevent her from claiming kinship to him. Worse—during that time of waiting, to have taken advantage of her trust. She could not know how hard he had tried to fight his attraction to her. He wished desperately to have some proof that his intentions had been good.

"You are quite sure, Wilfrid, that there was no record of a Payley—any Payley—in those church records?"

Wilfrid gave a sympathetic shrug. "Sorry, dear boy, but no. I can truthfully state that no such record remains in Cuckfield whether it ever existed or not."

"No mention, either, of the name Trevelyan?"

"I am sure if there had been, I should have noted it."

"Of course." Richard heaved a sigh. So he would have nothing with which to comfort Selina except for his own apologies. He would be proud to offer to pay for Augustus's schooling, but her pride was such that he expected she would refuse him. He would hate to resort to telling her about the conditions under which the King's Scholars lived, but eventually he would be forced to. And then, though she might accept his aid for Augustus's sake, she would never forgive him for persuading her to do so.

The pull of Selina's warm body, her glow and innocence still drew him strongly. He wanted nothing more than to pursue her into the house, to make her listen to him and see reason. To take her in his arms and kiss her anger away—

No. Richard stopped himself from thinking such things. She would not want his embraces now. If he knew Selina, she would hurl a pot at him the moment he showed his face at the door.

But he could not let that danger prevent him from speaking his apology as soon as possible.

"Richard," Wilfrid asked, "shall you be returning to London now? If so, I must beg a lift from you."

Wilfrid's plea damped Richard's plans.

"How did you come to Uckfield?" While listening for Wilfrid's response, Richard reached up to run his fingers through his hair and found it still full of hay. Selina's sweet scent seemed to cling to his hands, to linger in the air of the barn. Richard doubted he could ever enter a stable again without thinking of her.

But Wilfrid was answering him and in a tone to make him feel more the villain. "I am ashamed to say that I was forced to come by mail coach part of the way, then to hire a gig. I am trying, sincerely trying to practice those little economies you suggested, Richard. But I cannot pretend to like them. No doubt but what they shall cost me my good health in the end. You can have no notion of the vulgar people who ride in such conveyances—every two out of three are afflicted with violent coughs or nervous spasms. You *shall* advise me, shall you not, of the first hint of such symptoms in me? I have an excellent medical man, whom I consult quite frequently, but even he must have his fears when a man of my advanced years is subjected to a mysterious disease. I was not so fortunate as to be gifted with your excellent constitution, Richard."

Richard had suffered enough of Wilfrid's prattle on top of his setbacks that morning. Such speeches could only make him desire to be gone.

"Wilfrid, if you will be so good as to wait for me a few moments, I will make my good-byes to Miss Payley."

"Dear me." Wilfrid's raised brows told him how foolish he thought that course of action to be. "It appears to me, dear Richard, that she has taken her farewell already."

"That may be," Richard said, absorbing this latest slap to his pride, "but I have not taken mine from her. I shall be with you shortly."

Leaving Wilfrid arguing helplessly in the barn, Richard marched off toward the house with angry, guilty, churned up feelings still clouding his head.

When he arrived at the door, he was met by Lucas, who barred his way.

"Sorry, but Mistress Payley says she don't want no visitors."

Richard did not want to get into a brawl, but he would be damned if he would take his marching orders from Lucas. He struggled to control his irritation. "I do not think your mistress regards me as a visitor, Lucas. If you will kindly step out of the way—"

"That's what I would've said, if anybody 'ad asked me." Scratching his head, Lucas refused to move aside. "But, fact is, she partic'larly mentioned you as someone she don't want to see."

A pounding rage, born of humiliation, rushed to his temples. Richard did not think he had ever suffered such a blow to his pride . . . if that was what he was feeling.

Confused, and suffering from a pain he did not recognize, he could only accede to Selina's wishes, hoping to find her less averse to hearing his explanation at a later date. He could not very well fight Lucas in front of Wilfrid, not after his cousin had reproached him. Richard did have some dignity to maintain. He had to remind himself of that.

But since he had come to the Grange it seemed, his dignity had been flung out the window along with his conscience. The latter had now returned with a vengeance. It was long past time to take up the first.

"Very well," Richard said, giving Lucas the look a

earl should give an underling. "You may tell Miss Payley that I shall call upon her at her earliest convenience."

Concealed from his view at the top of the stairs, Selina heard the severe tone in Richard's voice. It wounded her, deep down where her heart had already crumbled into pieces, like broken glass that nicked and sliced her with every turn.

To learn that she had offered herself, heart, body, and soul, to a man who had deceived her was the greatest pain she had ever suffered, greater even than her sorrow on the loss of her parents. For this blow, not even Augustus's love or his need for her strength could act as a shield. She had suffered a wound straight through her heart, which nothing at all could ever heal. And at the moment she could not even summon the fury she knew she needed temporarily to fill it.

Richard tried again the next day, but was greeted at the door by Augustus.

"Is it true?" the boy asked with a droop to his features. "Are you truly the Earl of Linton?"

"Yes." Richard braced himself. "I am afraid so."

"Then, you did not come to the Grange to buy trees."

"No, although"—at Augustus's calm demeanor, Richard gave a sad smile—"I would be grateful for the chance to buy some now. If," he added, "you would be willing to sell them to me."

Augustus looked uncomfortable. "I would, I suppose, but my sister might not wish for me to do it."

"That's quite all right, Squire. I don't want to get you in trouble with your sister, but perhaps, if she would see me, I could ask her myself."

"Selina is not here."

The boy's words stunned Richard. Until that moment

he had not realized how much he had been counting upon seeing her today and asking for her forgiveness. He had thought of nothing else throughout last night or all this morning. He had resisted all Wilfrid's attempts to make him see reason and leave Uckfield behind them.

And in the end Richard had lost his temper with his cousin and sent him packing.

"What do you mean, she is not here?" he asked Augustus.

Augustus cast him a slanted glance, as much as to say that Richard could not be trusted to know.

Richard winced at the boy's honest regard. "I know that my behavior must seem reprehensible both to you and to your sister. I hardly understand it myself. But, Augustus"—Richard hardly knew where to start—"all I can say is that, for the past two weeks, I have been earnestly trying to discover some means by which I could be of service to you."

A light in Augustus's eyes told Richard that the boy wanted desperately to believe him, but all he uttered was, "Selina said you were posing as our friend in order to keep us from proving our kinship to you."

"I had gathered she thought something of the kind. However, she is wrong."

"I still can't tell you where she is."

Richard swallowed his frustration. "Did she leave you alone with the work?"

"Lucas is here."

"Ah. Yes, Lucas." Richard fought to control his sense of irony. Lucas had proven to be more trustworthy than he. "I would be happy to help myself, until she returns."

"No, my lord, you may not."

Augustus's mode of address hurt Richard. But a day ago they had been friends.

Augustus looked down at his shoes and studied their

tips. "My sister told me that I should send Lucas for the constable if you refused to leave."

"I see." Nothing would be served by Richard's staying here now, not until Selina's temper had cooled at least.

Richard made the boy a bow, but refrained from making long farewells, for he meant to return.

As he started to leave, a disturbing thought came into his mind. He swung rapidly around. "Augustus—you would tell me, would you not, if your sister's disappearance had anything to do with Romeo Fancible?"

The squire's puzzled look reassured him long before a light dawned in Augustus's eye. "No"—the boy nearly blushed—"it has nothing at all to do with Romeo."

"Well, in that case," Richard said more firmly, "I shall leave a message for you to give to your sister. You may remind her that she made me a promise with respect to that gentleman, and I expect her to keep her word."

Augustus seemed befuddled again, but without further questions, he agreed to pass Richard's message along.

The road to London seemed very much longer, far colder, and much more lifeless than it had on Richard's journey out to Uckfield.

The bustle of Bond Street, the haughtiness of St. James's, and the pretentiousness of every rider in the park struck him as both alien and artificial. He felt as if he had been living almost in another time, before such things as Almack's and balls, phaetons and routs, had ever been invented.

His first days back, he was far too busy to examine his emotions closely. He was bombarded by requests for his time from everyone from his steward to his housekeeper, not to mention his anxious secretary, who had been obliged to make decisions on his own about which social engagements Richard would be likely to attend. Advised by Wilfrid of his cousin's impending return, the poor man had sent out various notes of acceptance for this or that ball or scheme, only to discover two days later that Richard did not wish to accept any of them. After begging his employer to reconsider at least some, the secretary was forced to concede.

Richard found that his coming home did not give him any degree of solace. To the contrary, after a few days passed, he felt, if possible, worse than he had ever felt before. The constant demands for his attention quickly wore him down, until he wished for nothing more than the peace and quiet he had discovered in Selina's cherry orchards.

Then, a letter arrived, bearing the seal of the College of Arms. Wondering if further evidence had been found to give Selina hope, he tore it open.

Its contents, however, had nothing to do with the Payleys' claim. The Garter had written:

> *. . . I am well aware that the ancient Pedigrees of Trevelyan state their descent through Valetort from Edmond, Earl of Cornwall, Son of Richard King of the Romans, Son of King John; and that the Arms ascribed to that Earl have been quartered by your Family; but recent research has uncovered the fact that the Earl died without Issue, and that the King was his Cousin & next Heir. It is probable that the Wife of Valetort may have been an illegitimate Daughter of Earl Edmond; but I have not been able to refer to any date for establishing even such an altered position.*
>
> *I enclose, therefore, a revised painting of your Arms and Crest, with the Martlets, erroneously inserted in the Calverly Achievement, transformed into Owls. . . .*

Richard came to the end of the Garter's letter and gave a sardonic laugh. He had marched down to Sussex to lecture Augustus on the sanctity of the Trevelyan name, only to discover now that its much vaunted royal blood—if, indeed, there were any—had come from the wrong side of the blanket.

Unfortunately he found little consolation in the irony. It had little effect on his present feelings, which were confused at best. He could only hope that a period of quiet would help him recover his equanimity.

White's, he discovered when he had fled to his club in desperation, was agreeably thin of company by day. Tucking a newspaper under his arm, Richard sought a deserted corner in which to read.

Soon, however, he put the paper down and resigned himself to the fact that solitude was not all he had been missing. As the words on the printed page stubbornly eluded him, a great sense of loss invaded his heart. All Richard could think of was Selina, the fire that flashed in her eyes, the way she raised her perfect chin when riled, the sheer vitality that radiated from her. He fought the memory of her body pressed eagerly against his, and trembled with yearning to fulfill the promise of what they had begun that day in her barn.

He indulged himself with fantasies, the pleasure he would get from treating her to every luxury, things she had never seen or possessed, but which had been his from the very moment of his birth. He wanted to dress her magnificent figure in silks and satins of the finest mode. And, more than anything else, he wanted to soften her bitter pride.

His daydreams were inevitably ruined by the recollection of the hurt he had done her. Before he could achieve them, he would have to secure her forgiveness. Richard was not used to doubting his own powers of persuasion, but worry over what he would do if Selina refused to pardon him tied his stomach in knots. Never before had a woman meant this much to him. The urge to keep and protect her had nearly turned him into a vicious brute. And the thought that Romeo's attractions—one of which was sure to be honesty—would now look more favorable than his own made him fret like a spirited horse in harness to get back to the Grange.

If he returned and found her at home, how long would it be before she could even contemplate accepting his apology? Selina was proud. So proud. She would not be quick to forget the wound to her pride.

She believed that he had concocted some devious plot to prevent her from claiming his name, that he had engaged in a nefarious scheme with Wilfrid. As ridiculous as such a suspicion might be, Richard knew his dishonesty had led her to form it. He could no longer defend it, for even though he had thought his motives decent at the time, he now knew how confused they had been. The shame of her accusation burrowed beneath his skin like a nettle, and the feeling was not relieved by the certainty of his motives now.

He wondered how long it would be before he could see her. Wherever she had gone, it could not be far, for she would not leave Augustus to manage by himself for long. The trouble was that he could not insist upon being received. Selina, in a fit of temper, was quite capable of having him called up before a magistrate for assault.

At the thought of waiting for her temper to cool, Richard grew terribly impatient. There ought to be something he could do to show her the worthiness of his intentions.

The notion that he might search the Cuckfield registers himself for an entry Wilfrid might have overlooked occurred to him. If Selina could be proven to be his distant cousin, she might be willing to forgive him. However—and this was rather a large *however*—she might be so angry with him now that she would refuse the connection.

Richard wished that he could get at the heart of her pride instead and take away the blight upon her own family's honor. But to do that, he would have to prove her father's innocence, which should be an impossible task.

Thinking back to his first impressions of Selina and Augustus, he was struck again by the improbability that two such fine people could have been bred and raised by a dishonorable man. With a spurt of conviction, Richard realized that he did not believe it even remotely possible.

And if he was so inclined, he realized with a spurt of hope, then William Payley must have had some contemporaries who believed equally in him.

Coming to his feet, Richard determined to ferret these friends out and to conduct his own inquiry. It should be quite simple to discover the details of William Payley's scandal. More than half of Richard's fellow club members would have gone to Eton. A great number of these would have been at Cambridge—even Wilfrid had spent time there. What better place to begin his investigation than here?

Striding toward the card room, Richard did some vague calculations in his head. If Selina was approximately twenty years of age, then her father would most likely be in his forties or fifties if he were still alive. Richard guessed he would have been close to thirty, at least, before marrying, for a man who had been stripped of his place in society would have taken longer to find a way to support a wife.

Richard reached the card room, where low voices and the faint smell of tobacco proclaimed that a few tables had already been made up. Scanning the faces of the players, Richard found someone he supposed to have gone to Cambridge.

A portly Lord Eppington waved a casual hand of greeting. At Richard's question he waxed at great length upon his own history, having been sent to university to be trained for government service, only to be so fortunate as to inherit a barony instead. Richard listened patiently to him, and was finally rewarded with a list of men he might approach who had been up at Cambridge some thirty years ago.

Richard thanked him, and before the day was out, he had spoken to more than a few of the gentlemen on the list, had whittled the others down, and had invited one promising prospect to dinner.

Sir Henry North, a mild-spoken diplomat in the Regent's service, had undoubtedly been intrigued to receive an invitation to dine from a peer he only knew by repute. He came on fairly short notice, however, upon being informed by Richard's secretary that his lordship wished to question him about a private matter, concerning an incident that had taken place many years ago.

Always a gracious host, Richard made sure that his guest had been superbly fed and had been treated to his extensive wine cellar before he broached the serious topic of the evening. In light conversation over their dinner, he had discovered Sir Henry to be a man of both keen intelligence and high integrity. He had also, Sir Henry himself confirmed, been a close boyhood friend of William Payley.

"Yes." Sir Henry nodded regretfully over his port, once the covers had been removed and the servants had withdrawn. He was dressed in black along the lines laid down by Brummell, and the hair at his temples had turned a dull gray. "William Payley was a close and valued friend. I have never ceased regretting the unfortunate incident that robbed me of his companionship."

He raised his eyes to Richard's. "Why do you ask of him, my lord?"

Richard leaned forward to pour his guest another glass of port. "I have recently become acquainted with William Payley's children," he said. "Finding them in distressed circumstances, I formed an interest in their behalf."

"I see."

Sir Henry's searching look belied his simple statement. A man of his perspicacity must wonder just what Richard's particular interest would be in two persons he could not be expected to know.

But Richard was not of a mind to admit anyone to his confidence yet. Not until he had spoken to Selina.

Addressing Sir Henry, he said, "So, if I understand you correctly, the incident at Cambridge caused you to sever your relations with William Payley?"

Sir Henry's brows shot up. "Not at all, though you may be surprised to hear it. It was Payley himself who decided he would no longer maintain contact with his former friends in order to spare them the embarrassment of association with an outcast." Again, that searching look sought Richard. "William was a fine gentleman. He had more than one friend willing to accept his version of the story."

"Which was . . . ?"

Sir Henry paused for a curious length of time. When at last he spoke it was with an embarrassed laugh. "My lord, I hope you will forgive me. But I cannot help wondering why you are posing these questions to me instead of to your own cousin."

Nothing he could have said could have surprised Richard more. "My cousin Wilfrid?" he asked. A vague sense of disquiet began to invade his being. "Why should Wilfrid have anything to say upon the subject?"

After a moment's pause, Sir Henry's face relaxed. "Then, you do not know of your cousin's involvement in the scandal?"

His question rocked Richard. He responded with a sharp shake of his head.

"I begin to see. . . ."

"Then, you are much more fortunate than I," Richard said quickly, "and I beg you to enlighten me at once."

"You would have been just a babe at the time, if even born. Forgive me, Lord Linton, if I have been mistaken in my notions, but apparently you were not aware that your cousin, Sir Wilfrid Bart, was a principal participant in the incident we have been discussing."

"A principal participant. Do you mean, Sir Henry, to say that Wilfrid was one of the gentlemen playing at cards with William Payley when he was accused of cheating?"

"No, my lord. That is not all I mean to say." Sir Henry faced Richard squarely. "Your cousin was one of the players, but he also was the gentleman who laid the accusation of cheating against my friend."

Richard felt the first quiverings of sickness deep inside his stomach. "I confess," he eventually said, "you have astonished me."

"Then, at this point, perhaps you would prefer to consult with your cousin about the incident."

Richard's laugh was bitter. "I think not, Sir Henry. When you hear that my cousin has denied all knowledge of William Payley or his family, perhaps you will understand why I would prefer to learn the details from you."

A look of deep satisfaction spread over Sir Henry's features. "Very well," he agreed.

Over the next many minutes, he reconstructed the circumstances of what had been only one of countless card games among the students of King's College, recounting a time when he and his friends had been both young and irresponsible. Listening to him now, Richard found it hard to believe that such a staid gentleman could ever have been so heedless, and he said so.

With an astute grimace Sir Henry conceded how much he had changed. "It was, in no small part, due to my friend's tragic fall that I became the sober man you see today. It did not escape me that if a fine chap like William could be ruined over a game of cards, then the same fate could always befall me. You must understand," he continued, "that William, no matter that he was a superior student, had picked up some rather inadvisable habits during his years at Eton. You know the reputation of the King's Scholars?"

"Indeed I do. A most interesting lot."

"Nevertheless, I did not then, nor shall I ever believe that William Payley cheated at cards."

"What do you believe happened, then?" Richard held his breath.

Sir Henry released his. "At the risk of offending you, my lord, I would suggest that another man at that table possessed the type of character that more readily lends itself to a lie."

"Wilfrid." Richard tried to keep his voice steady, but the anger he was feeling at this moment made him want to spit the name.

"I am sorry to say it"—Sir Henry shook his head—"but, my lord, I have to think it. You see"—he seemed puzzled by something—"your cousin had taken a strong dislike to William Payley, almost upon first meeting, which was strange when you consider that some relation existed between them."

"Relation?" Sir Henry's words made Richard churn inside. "To what relation do you refer?"

"That I cannot tell you. Only that William had

mentioned to your cousin that they had some family connection or other, which Wilfrid at first seemed perfectly willing to acknowledge. Before too long, however, his behavior changed, and he went about refuting any hint of a connection."

"Curious," Richard said, though his mind had leapt rapidly ahead.

What else could inspire Wilfrid to deny a relative if not the possibility that his own inheritance might be weakened?

"Of course," Sir Henry continued regretfully, "there is nothing that can be done to rectify matters now."

"No. Wilfrid is not likely to confess." Though with his jaw clenched tightly, Richard promised himself he would force his cousin into a confession if he had to strangle one out of him.

Sir Henry sat back in his chair and sipped his port. The room was silent for a while, but then he ventured, "It would afford me some satisfaction to know that William's children were being cared for. If you will make me a gift of their direction, Lord Linton, I should be most happy to do something for them."

Richard knew a question lurked behind Sir Henry's statement. A feeling of humility tempered his hope when he replied, "I would be happy to give it to you, sir. However, you may rest assured that William Payley's children will never want for anything again."

Chapter Eleven

*H*urt and angry, Selina had not waited to see whether Richard would return. Though a part of her ached desperately to hear his reasons for the deceit, she refused to give him the chance to slip past her defenses. The circumstance of his coming so soon after her application to the Garter, his neglecting to give his name, and his cousin's seeming inability to trace their family link were much too convenient for coincidence. Plainly he and Sir Wilfrid Bart had conspired to prevent her from laying claim to their name.

The fact that she had only done so in order to secure her brother's place at Eton had not dissuaded them from their design. Selina supposed that the elegant Lord Linton had not believed a penniless girl like herself would have such a selfless motive. But with his own poor conscience to guide him, he must have feared she would try to make demands upon his purse as well.

The thought that Richard suspected her of being a fortune hunter made her flush with wounded pride. She would rather die than beg for money. But apparently Richard had not been able to see this aspect of her character. What he had seen, and had been quick to turn to his advantage, was a girl only too eager for his kisses.

The shame of her eagerness in his arms made Selina weep inside, but she refused to be cowed by what was past. Her ready anger, her pride's best ally in her troubled life, surged to bolster her resolve. No one would ever be permitted to see how foolishly she had allowed herself to be duped.

And no one would catch her waiting at home to discover whether Richard would come back to explain his perfidy or whether he would abandon Uckfield and her without a parting glance.

Before the sun had set on Richard's back, Selina had already made her plans. Since Richard's emissary was not to be believed, she would have to find her own proof of Joshua Payley's marriage to Anne Trevelyan.

Leaving Augustus alone to manage the farm was her only cause for concern, but she knew that her pride would accept no other solution, and Augustus assured her that he would call upon their neighbors if any crisis arose.

Unfortunately these words reminded her of the promise she had made in the barn, that she would never marry Romeo Fancible. Brushing a hasty tear from her eye, Selina told herself that promises to traitors need never be kept, but it took all the strength she possessed to hide her misery from Augustus. She scribbled a hurried note to the vicar, asking him to watch over Augustus in her absence, and left the Grange the next morning, knowing she had done all she could to protect her brother.

The stagecoach would be passing through Uckfield before dawn. Unwilling to risk meeting Richard at the inn, Selina made Lucas drive her in the wagon as far as the road to Hayward's Heath, where the coach might be flagged down. Before he left her shivering in the bitter cold of a February morning, she threatened him upon pain of dismissal not to leave her brother to cope alone, and assured him that if he did not make all haste back to the Grange, he would feel her wrath upon his back the moment she returned. Surprisingly the scapegrace seemed to take the responsibility of guarding his young master more seriously than she ever would have believed, which gave Selina one reason for comfort.

The stage, when it came, was crowded and noisy and redolent of onions. But a large, matronly woman insisted there was room for one more, and argued with the other passengers until they made a place for Selina on the seat. Wedged between this woman's soft, warm body and the sharp elbow of a man who was far less charitable, Selina prayed she would find what she sought in Cuckfield.

Not knowing whom she would have to face, she had brought the valentine along with her, safely tucked inside the deep pocket of her cloak.

She did not dare to read it. The sentiment in those words would shake her fragile defenses, and she could not afford to give in to her sorrows now. Until this moment, when her own heart was in tatters, she had not known how much those lover's words had tempted her to believe in love. But now she could not think of them without remembering Richard's base deception.

Doubts about that other couple's feelings naturally followed. Had one person been loved and the other one spurned? Had Joshua Payley laid bare his heart to a Trevelyan only to have it trod into the dirt, too?

With a sharp shake of her head, Selina determined to discover the truth, no matter how long it would take her, though the pitifully few shillings in her purse gave her decision the lie.

The slow pace of the stagecoach in winter brought her into Cuckfield at about dark. Like most villages, Cuckfield seemed to possess only the one parish church, and though the window shade in the stage had been drawn, Selina did not think they had passed any others since leaving Hayward's Heath. The coach had stopped a number of times along the route, either to let a passenger down or to take another one up, and she had taken the opportunity on each occasion to peer outside. Nothing had greeted her gaze but open heath, unrelieved by villages or farms.

If the information she sought did not rest in Cuckfield Church, Selina knew she would have no choice but to return home. She did not have the money of a Wilfrid Bart to hire a carriage to take her from village to village. And she dare not spend their last resources seeking after a truth she could not be certain of.

The stage let her down in the street not far from the church. With a shiver Selina clasped her cloak tightly about her shoulders. Inured to the cold by a life of work outdoors, she was dismayed by the chill she felt now as she made her way inside.

The church was not as empty as one might have expected. An elderly woman had come to sweep out the nave. When asked, she identified herself as the vicar's housekeeper, and when Selina explained that her errand would require her to search the parish registers, the woman offered to notify him of her visit at once.

It was fortunate, Selina decided later, that the Cuckfield Church was so blessed. She might easily have found herself in one of the many churches with no clergyman at all or in one where the vicar was shared with several others. As it was, the Reverend Mr. Stanhope lived but a stone's throw away in a tidy vicarage, and he appeared to be at home.

Invited into his study, she was relieved to find a stooped, gray-haired gentleman with a scholarly air, who came instantly to his feet. His bow, though slightly wobbly and hardly polished, clearly ignored the unfashionable cut of her clothes.

To say that he was surprised by Selina's visit would be putting it mildly, but his first gentle words made her tense.

"My, my," he exclaimed in a soft, pleasant voice as he took her offered hand. "This is most unexpected and most, most unusual. To think of having two visitors in the same week, and with the same purpose, mind you! Which is not at all to imply that either visit is unwelcome at all. No, no. Quite the contrary, in fact. A merely unexpected pleasure."

"Another person has come, asking to see the parish registers?" Selina knew at once he must be speaking of Wilfrid, but she wanted to be very careful about what she said.

"Yes, a most elegant gentleman. Quite turned out in the latest mode, I suppose, though I am hardly an authority upon the subject of clothes." Reverend Stanhope spied a spot of ink on one of his fingers and wiped it off with a linen handkerchief drawn from his coat pocket. "It is simply rare indeed for anyone in Cuckfield to sport quite the . . . degree of *color*, one might say, affected by the gentleman."

"Did you catch this gentleman's name? I suppose he might have been upon the same errand."

"His name?" Reverend Stanhope appeared flustered by the question. "Do you know, my dear, I do not believe he gave me his card. Nor, if I recollect, did he bother to name himself." He gave her an apologetic smile. "You see, I was so surprised—really quite put off my stride, as it were, by his quite unexpected appearance—most, most unusual to see such a turned-out gentleman in these parts—that I do not think I thought to ask for it."

Selina could tell by the strong impression the man had made on the vicar that he must indeed have been Wilfrid in his dandy's clothes.

The Reverend Mr. Stanhope, however, seemed to be reminded by her question to preserve the formalities now. He raised one inquiring brow her way.

Selina curtsied again and introduced herself.

"Payley. Payley," the vicar mused, turning her name over on his tongue, before his eyes lit. "I knew that name sounded familiar. This parish was quite peopled by Payleys not so many years ago. Though"—he corrected himself—"my concept of years may not be quite the same as one so young as yourself, not steeped in antiquities to the degree that I am."

Selina could not restrain a smile at his turn of phrase, though his words had made her heart skip a beat. "And what might the phrase mean to a gentleman steeped in antiquities, such as yourself?" she asked.

The vicar chuckled in a deprecating way. "Oh, I daresay, a century or two would not seem very long. But, you have a purpose for coming, if I am not much mistaken." He invited her to take the chair beside his desk. "I shall bring the registers to you. I am afraid there is more than one volume. It might be helpful if there were any particular date you had in mind."

Finding herself quite willing to trust such a kindly gentleman, Selina told the story of the valentine. When he asked whether she had brought it, she pulled it from her deep cloak pocket.

Mr. Stanhope looked it over with a pair of crooked pince-nez perched on his nose. "Most remarkable," he muttered with a scholarly tone of interest. "Yes, one would think the seventeenth century, both by the spellings and the intricate hand, wouldn't one? And remarkable as it seems, our register has survived since those troubled times." He gave her a sharp, conspiratorial look over his lenses. "Hidden, you see, throughout the Protector's reign. Would to God, we could find some more appropriate title for such a wretched villain! Protector, indeed!

"Though"—he shrugged and sighed—"history must be preserved, I suppose."

Surprising her with this angry aside—which, Selina guessed, must not be an entirely unexpected sentiment for a man of his beliefs—he handed her back the valentine. Then he said, "If you will be so good as to wait, I shall bring that volume to you."

"Was that the same one requested by the other gentleman?"

"Oh, dear me, no. He asked for them all. Said he would not require my assistance in the least."

"I see," Selina said, but her pulse had already started an agitated tattoo as she wondered what Wilfrid had found. There was nothing she could do but read the registers and see, but the fact that Wilfrid had not given the vicar his name seemed rather suspicious.

A pair of simple explanations did present themselves. The vicar might be so absentminded that he had merely forgotten Wilfrid's name, or it was possible that Sir Wilfrid Bart was so arrogant, he had seen no reason to supply it. But Selina's instincts strongly urged her not to trust Richard's cousin or his story.

The vicar returned presently with a large, ancient tome, which he insisted upon dusting with his own ink-stained handkerchief. Then, before leaving her to peruse it, he begged her to rise so that he might draw her chair closer to the fire. "For if you will forgive my mentioning it, my dear, I could not help noticing that your hand was rather cold, and there is such a nasty draft from the windows. . . ."

As he fussed about her, making sure that she was comfortably settled and offering her a cup of tea, Selina could hardly keep tears from welling in her eyes. The dear man had remarked the chill of her fingers, but seemed perfectly willing to ignore the red and calloused look of her hands, which would have sunk her beneath the notice of many a less charitable gentleman.

By the time he had left her to go in search of his housekeeper to beg a tea tray for her, darkness had fallen. Selina did not know where she could possibly spend the night, but she thought Reverend Stanhope could be trusted to find her a place.

Putting that worry behind her, she started through the big tome, turning the stained and tattered pages with reverence.

It was not long before she came across the surname Payley tied to various and sundry given names. Mysterious ancestors, she supposed, whom she did not know. They were repeated one after the other in birth, marriage, and death. Some deaths hard on the heels of their baptisms, others trailing many years behind.

When she discovered the baptism of one Joshua Payley in 1633, her heart leapt with hope. With trembling fingers she leaned forward to look for a date that would correspond to his young manhood, but after flipping the succeeding pages back and forth a number of times, she could not seem to find any entries between the years 1637 and 1662.

Frustration raised a lump in Selina's throat and curled her fists into angry balls. Whether or not Cromwell had managed to defeat all his enemies in the years of his rule, it seemed he had destroyed enough to spoil her hopes now.

By the time the vicar intruded upon her silence to ask whether he could be of any assistance to her, Selina had composed herself. "No, I thank you, sir. It would appear that my ancestor was wed during a time no records were kept."

"Dear me, how odd," Mr. Stanhope uttered mildly. "I can recall no period in which *some* record or other was not kept. I cannot pretend that all my predecessors were men of letters, but at least in matters of the register, they seemed to take their duties seriously enough."

Selina sighed inwardly. The vicar, for all his sweet intentions, could not possibly expect to know how well all the records had been kept. "I am afraid, in this instance, there was no predecessor, or if there were, he must have feared for his life. No records at all were kept for a period of more than twenty years."

His head jerked up at that, his seemingly habitual expression of foggy benevolence changed to one of deep concern. "But that cannot be, my dear. Oh, dear me, no. You must be mistaken." He reached for the volume. "May I . . . ?"

Selina wearily handed it over. It was plain to her what had occurred, which would make it useless for her to go to another church with her search. She had found Joshua Payley's parish, the record of his birth, and even his death in 1688. But there was nothing in between—a period of great strife, when Cromwell's men were attacking both established church and pagan custom. And there would be nothing Selina supposed she could find without tracing Miss Anne Trevelyan's family. And she had no clue as to where to begin on the Trevelyan side.

Mention of some Trevelyans had been made in the parish register, but there was nothing to say whether the name she was looking for had come from this branch of the family or another.

"Dear me!"

The vicar's strong tone grabbed her attention.

"This is not right." He shook his head. "It is not right at all."

"Vicar?"

Raising his troubled gaze to hers, Reverend Stanhope spoke sternly. "My dear, it would appear that some pages have been cut from this book."

Doubting, Selina said, "But I saw no pages torn." She went to stand beside him. "See. All the edges are clean."

"Yes, and they would be if a whole section of pages had been cleanly extracted from the binding. See how loose it is." The vicar shifted the binding back and forth in his hands. "You can tell that something is missing, else the threads would not be so exposed."

Selina could see what he meant. With the pages folded and sewn in sections, she would not have noticed that a whole section were missing if it had been completely cut out. "That would explain why so many years were gone. A page might contain a year of events—perhaps even two or three—but a whole section would have many years' recordings."

He nodded, and Selina was surprised to see anger again on his kind old face. "This is most reprehensible. To deface a valuable document such as this—and church property, too! Why, the man should be drawn and quartered!"

"But, Reverend Stanhope—how can you be certain when it occurred, if indeed, you can be certain it occurred at all?"

"Because I know these registers were complete. I read them all the year I took over as vicar of this parish."

Selina stared. His indignation was immense. And his certainty was not to be denied.

"You read them all?" Her question was not one of disbelief, but fascination.

"Yes, I—" Her interest had made him suddenly self-conscious again. "I have already admitted to being something of an antiquarian, and as such, you must realize, I find it impossible to overlook any document over a particular age. You will think that a church register might not afford much in the way of an intellectual stimulus— and indeed, one would not take the time to commit one to memory as one might a more intriguing document—but I can assure you, Miss Payley, that I would have remarked and remembered a gap of some twenty years."

With a sinking heart, all the more defeated by the particular depth of Richard's perfidy, Selina had to acknowledge the truth. The evidence of her ancestor's marriage to a Trevelyan had existed. It had been destroyed quite thoroughly, and most efficiently by Wilfrid, probably when his gentle host had gone in search of refreshment for him.

Tired and drained, Selina tried to marshal her fury, but it abandoned her when needed most. There was nothing she could do, but return to Uckfield with her tail between her legs and live as they always had lived. She might work her fingers to the bone and her back to the shape of a gnarled oak tree beaten down by the wind, but she would never be able to better their situation. And she would never be able to send Augustus to school as he deserved.

Gathering the remnants of her dignity, which now lay in tatters around her, she thanked the Reverend Mr. Stanhope for his help and expressed her sorrow that a family affair of hers could result in damage to his parish register.

"There, there, my dear. It is not your fault."

When Selina would have confessed that it was her application to the Garter that had started the series of events in motion, he would not hear her self-blame. "No, no, my dear," he said, closing the register with a softly final thud. "It is very easy to see who is deserving and who is not. When you try to save men's souls on a frequent, if not daily, basis, you soon come to recognize the good from the bad.

"But, come"—he began to usher her from the room—"Mrs. Simmons, my most excellent housekeeper, has made you up a room and a bed. For, if I am not much mistaken, you have traveled too far today even to think of returning tonight. And dinner in your room on a tray . . . ?"

With the fatigue of hopelessness, Selina allowed the gentle man to shepherd her to rest.

Richard would have been cheered to know that someone at least was taking care of Selina in his absence. The pleasure of telling her of his discovery, which he hoped to have soon, would have to wait on his more immediate task, that of extracting a full confession from Wilfrid.

To that end, he summoned Wilfrid in a note that left no room for misinterpretation, though Wilfrid might try to pretend it was nothing more than a friendly invitation. He appeared the next morning, unrepentant, and Richard saw it would not be easy to shake him from his complacency.

The skin on Wilfrid's face was a shade of delicate pink, achieved, no doubt, by the liberal use of rouge. Richard promised himself that by the time their chat was concluded, it would appear a sickly green instead.

"I had a most enlightening conversation the other evening," Richard began in a cordial voice, leaning back in his chair. "With a friend of yours, I believe."

"Really, dear boy?" Betraying only a mild interest, Wilfrid played with a fan he had tied to his wrist. "I did not know that you was become intimate with the Carlton House set?"

"Oh, this is not one of Prinny's friends. And I daresay 'friend' was not the precise word I should have used. He was rather an old acquaintance of yours. One of your schoolmates, in fact."

A pause in Wilfrid's fidgeting told Richard he had hit his mark. "An old playmate of mine? Are you sure?"

"He seemed to think so. Sir Henry North was his name."

Braced already, Wilfrid barely winced before trying to cover his recognition. "North? Sir Henry North?" he repeated, addressing the air. "I suppose there might have been someone by that name at Eton, but I cannot be absolutely certain after so many years."

"Come come, now, Wilfrid. You tried that trick once before. Do you recall? When I inadvertently showed you the letter from the Garter and you disavowed all knowledge of William Payley."

An ugly smile spread slowly over Wilfrid's features. "There, now, Richard, is where I am afraid you will find you are quite mistaken. I never disavowed a William Payley, for I was not asked about a William Payley. I believe Augustus was the name mentioned in the letter I read."

The sheer effrontery of his pose made Richard seethe inside, but he smiled, hiding his emotions. "Yes, I quite see. You always were the truthful one."

"Precisely."

"To the letter, in fact, if not to the intent. Oh, you're a clever one, Wilfrid. I even believed your quite touching testimonial of your devotion to my family name. Enough, in fact, to send you racing up to Cuckfield. I suppose it was rather like setting the fox to watch the hens."

Richard's outward appearance of amusement had achieved the effect he wanted. Wilfrid was gazing at him smugly, obviously content with his work. If he had been smoked, which he obviously had, then he wanted to enjoy his triumph.

"Why did you so particularly wish me to eschew that connection, Wilfrid?" Richard casually asked. "Did you object so strongly to sharing a few hundred pounds? After all, Miss Payley had only made her application to the

Garter in order to secure her brother's acceptance as a King's Scholar. But, of course, you could not know that."

Wilfrid's smile fell from his face, but was soon replaced by another, just as smug. "You are quite right, cuz. If I had known, I might not have been quite so energetic in your cause. But, do you know, I think my efforts were not wasted at all. No"—he paused—"the more I think about it, I am sure they would have been needed at some point, so it is well it were done."

"You refer, I suppose, to the fact that some evidence certainly existed linking the Payley name to mine."

Wilfrid inclined his head. "It did exist . . . but I am afraid I must inform you that, sadly, it no longer does." To this minute he had shown no contrition at all.

"But why should that disturb you?" Richard made his question sound as if his interest were academic. "It is true that I would have felt a strong compulsion to help William Payley's descendents out of their current misfortune. But I hardly think that would have alarmed you. As eager as you are to inherit my estate, you must know how easily it could support another dependent or two."

Controlling the impulse to examine his cousin as if he were a particularly vile form of asp, Richard waited, tensed, for Wilfrid's explanation. He had seen a flicker of hesitation in Wilfrid's eyes, but now they appeared to glow with a curious satisfaction.

"Do you mean to say, dear cuz, that you have not yet tumbled to the exquisite truth?" Wilfrid's lip curled in a sneer. "Deary me. I must say, I am disappointed in you when I had been thinking you such a downy one."

Richard felt strangely impervious to Wilfrid's contempt. He found it was hard to be squashed by an asp.

"I feel sure you mean to enlighten me," he said, letting a note of admiration steal into his voice. "That is the reason I invited you here today. There must be some reason why you would go to such lengths first to ruin a relation, then to deny him."

"But of course there was a reason." Wilfrid's tone told Richard he had been incredibly dense. "When have you ever known me to exert myself to no benefit?"

"To yourself?" Richard did not skip a beat. "Never."

"Precisely, dear boy. Though, if you will forgive me, I think I shall leave off with the 'dear boys' from now on." Wilfrid sighed. "After so many years of pretending, I find this feigned affection has taken years off my life. If you only knew. . . ." Wilfrid smiled as if with profound relief. "When I think of the times I have lied and said you were an adorable child, when the truth was quite, quite the opposite. I have always despised children, but you, dear Richard, were rather loud. And boisterous. You even had the effrontery to ask me—your 'Uncle Wilfrid' as you called me then—to make a horse out of my leg for you to ride on." At the memory Wilfrid shuddered.

Richard allowed him his moment of spite, only mildly surprised by the depth of Wilfrid's hatred for him. He was much more astonished to hear it expressed so openly. Though Richard had known that little love existed between them—Wilfrid was far too eager to inherit Richard's fortune to have much affection for him—Richard still thought it strange for Wilfrid to divulge this so completely and with so little provocation. He could only assume that something had made Wilfrid feel extraordinarily secure to do so now.

Richard waited a moment before saying mildly, "These reminiscences are all quite touching, Wilfrid, but could we return to the topic at hand? Why did you seek to destroy William Payley?"

"Ah, yes." Wilfrid smiled a chilling smile that Richard felt like wiping off with a facer. "Well, if you will promise not to tell anyone, I shall be happy to let you in on my little secret.

"After all," he continued, ignoring Richard's failure to respond, "it would be only your word against mine. And, in case I have to remind you, dear cuz, I have one friend at least—a rather influential friend if his palace at Brighton is anything to go by—who would rather believe *me* than you."

Richard's expression must have betrayed his sudden understanding, for Wilfrid shook his head with mock sadness. "You should have had the wits, Richard," he said, "to quit the Whigs as soon as Prinny ever did."

Richard stared at Wilfrid grimly, aware of the import of his words. Wilfrid thought himself as safe from public censure as anyone could ever be. Anger churned inside Richard at the thought of the Regent's misplaced favor, but he was not through with Wilfrid yet.

"You have made your point. But now I confess I am all agog to hear why you took such great pains to conceal the connection."

"There is not much to tell." Wilfrid waved a careless hand. However, his lips were parted in an avaricious smile, his eyes closed to mere slits as he said, "Only that William Payley's ancestor, Miss Anne Trevelyan, was the elder sister of my very own female ancestor."

Feeling suddenly as if a piece of gauze had been lifted from before his eyes, Richard nodded slowly. "Of course," he said in a wondering tone. "That would be the ancestor on whom your claim to my fortune is based."

"Precisely. So"—Wilfrid inclined his head—"you see that without my interference, a higher claim could easily have been asserted by those farmers of yours. Is it not fortunate that my branch of the family had the good sense to claim the connection so many years ago? To claim and register it with the Garter? William Payley's family deserves to be punished for such inattention to their own self-interest. But do you know"—Wilfrid's tone implied there was a lesson to be learned from this episode—

"when I think about the insufferable airs William Payley used to affect, I think the error was due to misplaced pride. Is it any wonder that pride is thought to be a grievous sin?"

Richard allowed his cousin to rattle on, though his hands trembled beneath his desk with the urge to strangle Wilfrid. And this desire came close to overwhelming him when he thought of the miserable life Selina had led.

The work and the pain, the fears about her future and her brother's, the humiliation and the indignity—all, it seemed, could be laid at his weaselly cousin's door.

Richard wanted nothing more than to make Wilfrid grovel in apology at her feet, which he planned to do symbolically, if not in fact. Thoughts of Selina's work-roughened hands, the chores she had been subjected to repeatedly, goaded him now as he stared at his cousin's smirk.

It was with this mixed pair of images before his eyes—Selina's relentless suffering versus Wilfrid's undeserved content—that his cousin's next words penetrated his brain.

". . . And you will undoubtedly thank me one day, Richard, for preserving you from such an undesirable connection. 'Pon rep! To think of the Earl of Linton being forced to give the nod to such a set of yokels. Why, the very thought—"

Never in his whole life had Richard felt the fury that surged in him at that moment. The pressure it built was such that he could no longer sit.

His sudden leap to his feet cut Wilfrid's words off short. Richard had the satisfaction of seeing a pale, sickly gray replace the bloom in his cousin's cheeks.

"Since we are being perfectly honest for once"— Richard delivered his words in a scathing tone—"I think you should know that it has been the glaring penance of my life that I should be forced to call such a worthless

175

piece of rubbish as you my heir." He took a deep, cleansing breath before proceeding. "Which, in fact, makes what I am about to announce to you so exquisitely gratifying."

Even as he spoke, a sense of satisfaction was slowly drowning his ire, much the way a shower of rain extinguishes a tree aflame, giving Richard the ability to enjoy the play of emotions across his cousin's face.

At his first words Wilfrid had risen indignantly in his chair, only to fall back with a look of foreboding as he absorbed Richard's last syllables. Richard would have delighted in giving him a tongue-lashing in the hope of watching him shrink by several inches, but he knew what he'd planned instead would strike Wilfrid a coup no mere scold ever could.

"It gives me the greatest honor to announce to you, Wilfrid, that I soon plan to have a new set of relations who will effectively wipe you out of the running for my succession."

"But"—Wilfrid sputtered in his chair—"I've already told you no evidence exists—"

Richard stopped him with a smile and an upheld hand. "That will no longer be necessary, I fear. Not when I plan on making Selina Payley my wife. And you need not concern yourself over your cousin Augustus, for he will be perfectly happy living with his sister and me as my long-lost heir."

"But Prinny—"

Richard quelled him with a scornful eye. "Even Prinny will not be able to refute the evidence of kinship I am sure Miss Payley's uncle will provide when I inform him of the circumstances of his brother's disgrace. Once he knows of my intention to wed his niece, I am sure he will be able to present some proof or other of his ties to the Trevelyans. After all, as you yourself have pointed out, we are not all so afflicted with the honor and pride of a gentleman like William Payley."

As Richard painted this scenario, he did it merely to torment his cousin, for he had no certainty at all that William's brother would have any proof of their ties. Richard's true plans for an heir fell along entirely different lines, but he would not mention these to Wilfrid. They would far better be discussed with Selina alone.

Eager to do just that, Richard did not wait to see how Wilfrid received his news before heading for the door. Upon making his announcement, desire had welled inside him to see Selina and to hold her in his arms. The relief of being free of Wilfrid, too, had buoyed him, but he feared his confident feelings were likely to desert him before he faced Selina with his apologies, so there was no time to be wasted now.

He paused at the door.

"And need I point out that your allowance is hereby permanently revoked, as is your permission to visit this house? Now, if you will excuse me, *cuz*—"

Instead of seeing Wilfrid out, Richard left him sitting there, his mouth hung open in abject horror as Richard closed the library door.

Chapter Twelve

*W*hen Richard returned to Uckfield that evening, he found it had an unusually festive air. Men and women from the country had swelled the ranks of villagers. In spite of the gathering dusk and a strong threat of chill, the younger set collected in doorways to boast or giggle with their friends.

Normally the unexpected appearance of an elegant traveling coach bearing the coat of arms of the Earl of Linton would have attracted a great deal of attention. But the villagers halted in their visiting only long enough for one good stare at Richard's impressive crest, before taking up where they had left off. Richard's arrival caused no more flurry than a leaf that has drifted onto a pond already rippled by stones.

To say, however, that Mr. and Mrs. Croft at the inn were stunned by their discovery of his identity would be to understate the case. The sight of Richard's intimidating retinue, from his lofty coachman to his haughty, exacting valet, nearly reduced the poor couple to tears. If Richard had not already known them, he would have seen at once that his hosts were not accustomed to entertaining visitors of such an elevated rank.

But Richard would not think of appearing among these people again under any other guise. If Selina chose to disappoint him, he wanted the world to know that she had received a very eligible offer from the Earl of Linton and had refused him.

Mr. Croft seemed particularly anxious to be reassured that he had done nothing during Richard's previous stay to offend. But Richard's calm politeness, and his evident pleasure in being shown to his former room, quickly laid the poor man's fears to rest. Then Mr. Croft's only lingering regret seemed to be that he could not give his honored guest the full attention he deserved.

"For, your lordship," Mr. Croft informed Richard proudly, "tonight it falls to me to collect this year's valentines and dole them out by lot."

Richard had been so intent upon his confrontation with Wilfrid that morning, he had overlooked the day's date, and on the road his thoughts had been consumed with the problem of how best to approach Selina. Now he realized with a start that it was indeed Valentine's eve, and the first glimmer of hope he'd had since leaving London lit a spark in his chest.

He urged Mr. Croft to give him the details of the celebration.

"Well, your lordship," Mr. Croft said, "it goes like this. All the youths and the young maids hereabouts place their names in my basket. Then it's up to me to see that they're fairly parceled out."

"A most ancient custom, I presume."

"That and it is, your lordship."

Richard knew from the experience of overseeing his own estates that ancient customs were more likely to survive in rural areas. And in Uckfield, where the people were rarely exposed to the changing fashions of London, people would assuredly hold fast to the old ways.

"So the youths of Uckfield must take their chance, must they, on whom their favor falls for the year?"

Mr. Croft surprised him with a cunning wink. "Oh,

there's always them what are sharp enough to get around."

"Is that so?" Richard smiled at his host's evident complicity. "Would you care to inform me by what method a man, who happens to be in love with a particular maid, might be assured that his valentine will be received by the proper hands?"

A hint of reluctance tinged Mr. Croft's honest face. "Well, your lordship, if I said that some delivers their own valentines themselves, I wouldn't be telling ye wrong."

"But . . ." Richard sensed that Mr. Croft had a better way. "You have a different suggestion?"

"Aye, sir, your lordship." In his enthusiasm Mr. Croft seemed to shed ten years at least. "There are some what likes to do it in a more—what ye might call—devious way."

At Richard's encouragement he continued, "It can be arranged with the man in charge, so to speak, that the valentine be given to the proper maid."

"Oh, it can, can it?" Richard chewed this bit of information.

As Mr. Croft only gave another wink, Richard asked, "And would a request for you to cater my own wedding feast be sufficient inducement to perform such a service?"

A smile such as Richard had never seen lit up his host's ruddy features. "Sure and it would be that, your lordship."

"Then, I must instantly beg of you some paper and ink, with the promise that your service will be available when required."

"Yessir!"

Selina was sitting at the kitchen table with Augustus when he asked if she would go into Uckfield for the Valentine's eve celebration.

Since returning to the Grange, she had immersed herself in work, refusing to speak about Richard or her trip, except to inform her brother of the failure of her search. His subsequent attempts to convince her of the paleness of his scholarly ambitions had brought a mist to her eyes, but Selina was determined to match his courage. She would not let her own suffering add to his disappointment, and resolved to spare him an awareness of the hurt Richard had done her.

The fact that she had forgotten about the day's festivities might have stirred his curiosity, since so little happened to alleviate the boredom of their lives. An outdoor dance with local musicians on the Uckfield green certainly should have claimed her attention.

But Selina had no wish to go. She could not look upon happy couples without reliving the pain of Richard's betrayal. That she should, even now, find it so hard to believe him capable of such treachery was a constant source of confusion to her.

Her reluctance to accept the apparent truth seemed inconceivable. Why she should be so unwilling to resign herself to the evidence of his villainy, she did not know. Yet, despite all her resolutions to put Richard firmly out of her mind, she had to confess that she dreamed of him still. At the slightest sound she would glance up, hoping to find him at her door, and she could not help feeling in her heart of hearts that the connection between them had been real.

Was it Richard's gentility that had tricked her? Or had it been his smile, which she had found so warm and comforting whenever it bathed her, that had robbed her of all common sense?

Now that she knew he had been born into the peerage, other memories of Richard as he'd lived among them had returned to bewilder her. Richard nearly breaking his back with the work she'd assigned him. Richard fencing with the pig. Richard patiently discussing Cicero with Augustus. And, the most painfully lingering memory of all, Richard as tender lover.

"Selina?"

Selina had forgotten that Augustus was waiting for her reply.

"No, love," she answered him, looking up with a false smile. "I do not think I shall go to the dance. However, do not let me stop you. It should amuse you to watch the people on the green."

"Why won't you go?"

Selina tried to make light of his question. "I simply have no time for such frivolity. The sheets must be mended, and I had particularly intended to stitch a new shirt for you this evening."

"The shirt can wait one more day. Please come."

His importunity preyed upon her sorrow in a way Augustus could not possibly know. Selina struggled against ready tears by forcing a laugh. "Very well, if you really must know the reason. I do not go because I refuse to put my name in Mr. Croft's basket."

"Why?"

"Why?" she repeated. "Because I am far too particular to accept just any valentine."

"Is that why you no longer come outside whenever Romeo comes to check upon Nero?"

His acuity stunned her.

"Yes," Selina replied evenly. "I suppose that is why." She started to explain that she must not encourage Romeo to call upon them since she had discovered she had no wish to marry him. But her explanation was cut short by his next exclamation.

"Oh, I forgot," he said, looking shamefully remiss. "I forgot to tell you what Richard said before he left."

Selina felt the pain of Richard's name as if she'd been stabbed with a knife, which was why she failed to stop Augustus in time to prevent him from saying more.

Augustus recited his words carefully, as if, having failed to mention the message before, he must make sure of getting it right now. "Richard said that you had made him a promise with respect to Romeo Fancible that he expected you to keep."

"He had the nerve to send me that message?" Yet, even as she spoke, Selina's traitorous heart was bounding with a hope she could not quell. So Richard *had* cared.

"Yes, but what did he mean?" Augustus asked with a frown.

"Nothing you should concern yourself with now." Rising from her chair, Selina tried to hide the jumble of feelings his words had aroused. "You should be going along before you miss the start of the dance. You will not want to be late in coming home for fear of being too tired to milk Clarissa in the morning. And, if you do *not* come home early enough to suit me, I shall fetch you."

With that gentle threat, Selina bundled up her brother and pushed him out the door before he could think of any other questions with which to torment her. Sometimes his very youth and innocence could do more damage to her wounds than her own conscience, which had refused to cease berating her. Even now it was chastising her for refining too much upon Richard's words. He had gone and not returned, so why should she try so stupidly to give his message some construction that might take away her injury?

That she had made up her own mind not to encourage Romeo Fancible had nothing at all to do with the promise she had made Richard. She had simply learned how unfair it would be to tie up the heart of a man she could never hope to love. Romeo had been a generous neighbor and friend. She had no right to abuse his affections as Richard had done hers.

After taking herself to task for nursing forlorn hopes, even for an instant, Selina briskly set to work upon the promised shirt, settling herself in a chair beside the fire. Before long, however, the warmth and the luxury of being alone made her succumb to wandering thoughts. Closing her eyes, she gave in to the sweet temptation to recall the feel of Richard's arms about her and the memory of that brief, fleeting instant when she had felt herself cherished and loved. With a burning pang in her throat, she acknowledged it would most likely be the only such time of her life. No matter how false those few moments—those wickedly, blissfully delicious few moments—had proven to be, she would always treasure them as such.

Her thoughts were so engaged when a knock at the door made her start. With the practice of the past few days, she quickly wiped the moisture from her cheeks and the pain from her eyes before reaching for the latch.

The sight of Mr. Croft on her doorstep startled her. She would have thought him much too busy with his valentines to call upon her at such an hour, which fleeting thought gave her a sudden fright.

A ready welcome vanished from her lips. "Is it Augustus? Has he been hurt?"

Mr. Croft gave a surprised chuckle. "Not the squire, miss." He gestured behind him with his thumb, and she saw with relief that her brother was there and fine. "He thought he'd come along o' me to see what I've got in here for you."

Mr. Croft held out the basket he always used to collect the villagers' valentines. "There's nobbut one left," he said a bit ruefully, "and I bethought myself of you out here at the Grange."

Selina tried not to show how his thoughtfulness had pricked her. "That is very kind of you, Mr. Croft, but I did not put a valentine into your basket, so it would not be just for me to receive one."

"Go on, miss," he persisted, practically pushing the basket into her hands. "I've taken care of all the other maids around, and I've still got this one left. You wouldn't have me return it to the gentleman and hurt his feelings, now, would ye?"

Something in Mr. Croft's coy manner struck Selina as suspicious, and a resultant feeling of dread swept through her. What if Romeo had concocted a ploy to direct his valentine to her? If he had, then she would suffer no more than she deserved for using him so.

A niggling thought that such a high degree of cunning would be far beyond his mental powers made her wince with guilt.

"Go on, Selina." Augustus stepped up and added his plea to Mr. Croft's, which made Selina anxious to be done with the whole unpleasant business as fast as possible.

She snatched the remaining valentine from the basket and said stiffly, "Thank you very much, Mr. Croft." Then, to prove to both witnesses that she had no interest in their game, she tore open the missive at once.

She had not remarked that it had been closed with an unfamiliar seal, as if a heavy signet ring had been applied to the wafer. But as soon as she broke it, this curious detail did strike her, causing her hands to falter in their task.

The handwriting, too, was unfamiliar. This did not surprise her, for she did not expect to recognize the hands of all her neighbors. What it did do at once was to comfort her on Romeo's score, for she had seen his writing too many times not to know it.

Then instantly a delicate sketch of two swans at the top of the page, their necks curved into the shape of a valentine, caught her eye. The dear familiarity of the words, even if they were in the current tongue and not the ancient form she had memorized, set her pulse to fluttering wildly. The knowledge that the poem could not have been reproduced without painstaking memory brought tears into her eyes, so that she could hardly read.

> "Most suitors choose their love by chance,
> Yet, I disdain to follow such a dance,
> But take my wisdom from the birds above,
> To plight my troth instead to truest love,
> That this one year shall turn to life
> When Valentine shall be my wife."

Selina did not need to see Richard's signature at the bottom to know who the note was from, but she could not keep herself from rubbing her thumb over it lightly.

Augustus broke in. "What does it say, and who is it from?"

Selina's speech was hampered by a painful lump in her throat, but when she found that she could speak, she turned to Mr. Croft instead. "Mr. Croft," she said, trying to still the quivering in her voice, "is the—the gentleman who wrote this missive still lodging with you?"

"Aye, and that he surely is, mistress. And would you believe it," he said eagerly, "if I told you that Mr. Lint, the one what was here before, is the Earl of Linton, as sure as I live and breathe? Ye could have knocked me and the missus down with a feather when we saw him, what with his coach and all them uppity servants of his."

Selina thrust her chin high in the air, feeling as if a sudden breath of life had filled her chest. "Actually, yes, Mr. Croft. Both my brother and I have been aware of that fact for many days now."

So Richard had returned to Uckfield, as himself. But,

Selina cautioned herself, she must not be quick to think he had done it for her, not when, if she was wrong, it would hurt her far, far too much.

"Do you have any idea why his lordship has come back to Uckfield?"

She almost hated herself for asking, but Mr. Croft, when he answered, gave her a knowing smile that made her heart want to leap with hope.

"No, he didn't mention his reasons to me exactly, I'm sure, being as how it's not rightly my business yet. But"—Mr. Croft touched the rim of his hat as he made his farewell—"I do suspect that his lordship'll be along o' here in the morning with his valentine's gift. Good evening to you, Mistress Payley."

The next morning, Selina refused to be caught waiting for Richard to claim his valentine. A night of worry, mixed with purposely stoked anger and a fair share of wistful thinking, had convinced her that she would be the greatest of all possible fools to pin any hope upon his message. That the Earl of Linton would want to marry someone who, although a lady by her bloodlines, was in reality nothing more than a miserable country lass, with the rough hands to prove it, and, moreover, of a size to terrify a horse, was patently absurd. Besides, if Richard had wished to marry her, he might have asked her anytime during those three weeks he had practically lived at the Grange.

Meanwhile, the eggs must be gathered, the pig fed, and the cow milked, even if it was Valentine's Day morning.

Selina set off for the chicken coop with purposeful steps, which slowed as the thought crossed her mind that Richard might not have had a good opportunity to express his feelings. She and he *had* been interrupted at a rather unfortunate point. And Selina had to admit that she might have made such a declaration nearly impossible by the attitude she had shown him the previous week. It was even probable that he had begun to think she would prefer to receive an offer from Romeo Fancible.

Remembering the wantonness of her behavior on the morning he had left, she thought he had likely been disabused of his ignorance on that score.

With this last thought in mind, she found it hard to go about her work without jumping at the slightest sound upon the drive. She could not help envisioning what might happen if Richard should indeed decide to claim his valentine.

By midmorning, when she had returned to the house and he had not yet come, Selina was in a rousing temper. So much so, that when Lucas came to the door to ask for his lunch, he was forced to retreat without uttering a word. And even Augustus, who had perceived his sister's agitation at breakfast and had a better notion of its cause, had chosen to work in the farthermost orchard.

Selina—who, by this time, had begun to curse all men roundly—glanced outside her bedroom window only a few minutes later and found the Earl of Linton sitting on a bench beside the barn, deep in conversation with her brother. He had left what appeared to be a luxurious traveling coach outside the gate, which explained her failure to hear its approach. He and Augustus must have walked up from the orchard, and had been sitting there, she knew not how long.

Richard was dressed in a dark gray morning coat that fit his shoulders to within a fraction of an inch. A high-crowned beaver sat stylishly upon his head. Wellington boots, with an impossible shine, nearly reached to his knees, and a pair of pale gray inexpressibles hugged his thighs.

All these details came to Selina in an instant. In the

next she was racing for her dressing table with a cry of panic. Giving an anxious look in the mirror, she took up her brush and began to thrash her hair to dislodge the dust of the morning's work, all the while wondering why Richard would speak to her brother instead of to her. She could not think clearly enough to answer her own question, not when her knees were quaking and her arms trembled as if she had just picked a ton of cherries.

By the time Richard finally knocked upon her door, Selina was able to descend the stairs with clean hands and face, a fresher dress, and a fair semblance of composure. She held her chin high in the air and carried her skirt delicately before her. She did not rush, because it would be most unseemly to rush, and because Richard had taken his own good time in coming.

The sight of his handsome face when she opened the door to him, the way his eyes lit upon seeing her, and the gravity of his demeanor tamed the rest of her fury. But Selina could not allow herself to show how very glad she was to see him. Whether he had schemed against them or not, Richard had hidden his true identity, and for that he must earn her forgiveness.

Richard removed his hat and bowed. Resisting the urge to throw herself into his arms, Selina stepped back and allowed him to cross her threshhold.

"My lord." Mindful of the dignity she must preserve, she curtsied.

"Selina." In a voice with a husky edge, Richard claimed her attention before she could invite him into her mother's parlor. "I have just asked your brother for leave to pay my addresses to you."

"You have?" It had not occurred to her that he might seek Augustus's permission. Joy filled her, and her heart began to take flight.

At the thought of her brother, however, Selina recalled the injury that had been done to him, and the habits of a lifetime intervened. She fought the urge to hear Richard's declaration, and bristled at him instead. "I wonder that you would choose such a course, my lord, when he believes you to have wronged him."

Richard winced. "Perhaps I stood less in fear of his response than I did of your tongue." His teasing note held more than a hint of truth.

At the reference to her temper, Selina let it flare. "And perhaps you should have, my lord, for as his sister I must see that no harm comes to him, which means I should never allow him to be bamboozled by a stranger. Which means I should have—"

"Hung me from the rafters like a ham?" Richard's eyes held a glint. "Sold me out of hand to the gluemaker?" He stepped threateningly toward her.

"Or had me rendered down for fat and baked into a pudding?" As Richard steadily stalked her, Selina backed into a corner, uncertain of his mood. His eyes looked fierce with passion, and she wondered if he had decided he would take no more lectures from her.

Then she caught a glimpse of something deep inside them as his voice turned soft. "Or would you have your way with me? I can assure you, I had far rather choose that punishment."

Selina heard herself whimper with the desire to embrace him and erase that fearful longing in his eyes.

"Oh, Selina, I've been so afraid you would never forgive me."

"I would, but for Augustus—"

"Your brother knows now that I had no other desire than to help him."

She started hopefully at his words. Richard took both her hands in his.

"I would have come to you much sooner," he said, raising them one at a time to his lips, "but there was something your brother had a right to be told, and I wanted to take care of that business first."

"What business is that?"

"I shall tell it all to you in good time, but first I've come to claim my valentine."

"That was—is—a very foolish custom, my lord."

"I do not think it so."

His moist breath was warming her fingers, taking away the sting of all her years of work. Selina was ashamed to note the way her hands had gone limp inside his, as if they had a mind of their own. She knew she should press him to justify his deeds first, but these stronger urgings had been so long denied.

Richard ran his lips across her fingers in a trail of soft kisses. Selina wanted nothing more than to close her eyes and sway blindly toward him.

"I mean to claim you for my own, you know."

"You do?" Selina could not make herself resist any longer. "For the year, you mean?"

"For this year, and forever." He drew her close until her breasts nearly touched his chest.

"If I had known what the date was when I set out, I would have brought you a gift from London. But I've hardly known my own name, my mind has been so consumed with you. By the way you looked with your hair spread out on the hay, by the way your eyes sparkle with life, by the enticing scent of you."

He dipped his face to her neck and breathed deeply, causing a thrill to run down her spine.

"Then," he went on with his lips buried near her ear, "when I conspired to make you my valentine and had to come up with a gift, I thought of one thing only. Just one very pitiful thing, indeed. But by all rights, Selina, it is already yours."

"What could that be?" she asked. The way Richard talked mystified her, but she never wanted him to stop.

"My family name." Richard pulled back for a minute to gaze into her eyes. "You are, indeed, descended from Anne Trevelyan, my dear. Moreover, Augustus is my rightful heir."

Shock made Selina's knees go weak, but Richard was there to catch her. His arms went about her and stayed.

"But—your cousin—"

"My cousin Wilfrid is a liar and a cheat. I already thought him beneath my notice, but when I sent him to Cuckfield to search the church register for you, I had no idea how despicable he truly was.

"You were right to suspect that he'd destroyed whatever evidence he could find. I got that much confession from him. And now I also know why. Your ancestor, Miss Anne Trevelyan, was sister to the lady through whom Wilfrid stakes his claim as my heir."

Selina must have looked as stunned as she felt, for after waiting for her response, which never came, Richard led her into the parlor and pressed her onto the couch. Before continuing, he took a place beside her, his hand still holding hers.

"You see, love, earldoms such as mine are so ancient as to be baronies of writ. They descend to heirs general, which means they can be inherited through the female line, provided there is no male heir. If I were to die, Wilfrid and Augustus could both claim my honors, though Augustus's claim should take precedence since his female ancestor was the elder of the two sisters."

"And your cousin knew all that." Selina understood in part now. "But how could he, when we did not know ourselves?"

Richard's gaze intensified. "There is much more to the story than you know. I am afraid he learned this from your father, though I doubt your father ever realized the stakes that were riding on their connection."

"My father!"

"Yes. They met at Cambridge. And, your father, unaware as I was of how base Wilfrid's character truly was, announced to Wilfrid upon meeting him that they were distant cousins. When Wilfrid discovered what such a relationship would mean to his own expectations, he did what he could to disavow the connection. Even going so far as to discredit your father entirely in the eyes of his peers."

Selina did not need to see the sympathy in Richard's eyes to guess what he meant. A realization was dawning, bringing with it a mixture of feelings, ranging from the deepest sorrow to the purest rage. It left her awash with impotence that she should have been so helpless to restore her father's honor in his lifetime.

Richard told her then about the incident at Cambridge, when Wilfrid had accused her father of cheating to force him from society, so that, in effect, William Payley would never be heard if he made a claim to Richard's fortune and title. Such a wealth of emotion as this story aroused could not be experienced without its share of tears, but Selina's feelings were greatly helped by the way Richard cradled her in his arms. Before long, her uppermost concern was that she had stained his shirtfront with so much blubbering.

"That's quite all right, love. You may blubber all you like," Richard assured her. "I doubt you will have much need in future to do so. I mean to see personally that you do not."

These words brought back the proposal he had made her earlier, which had a wondrous effect upon her sorrow.

"But"—Selina did not know where Augustus stood now, and she would never let her own needs come before his—"you say your cousin has destroyed the evidence of a marriage. Doesn't that mean that Wilfrid will still inherit?"

Richard sighed. "It would be hard to prove Augustus's superior right to the Garter's satisfaction without a public and legal confession from Wilfrid, which, I can assure you, we are not likely to get. And, as my worthless cousin has pointed out to me, if it comes to a question of his word against mine, the Regent, who happens to be an intimate of his, is unlikely to throw his considerable weight in my corner."

"Then, what can we do?" Selina could not bear the thought that the man who had ruined her father's life would win this underhanded battle, as well.

While they'd been talking, she had stayed nestled inside Richard's arms, and now he gave her a squeeze.

"Oh, I think we have more than one ace to play," he said.

When Selina peered hopefully up at him, she found he was grinning. "I've already informed Wilfrid of my intention to adopt Augustus, and though he cannot inherit my title, I mean to settle at least one piece of property on him immediately. Then, if it comes to a question of one or the other of them inheriting, I will be sure to leave the bulk of my estate to your brother. You need never worry about his welfare again."

"Then, he can go to Eton?"

"To Eton and Cambridge and beyond. Whatever the boy wants."

"Oh, Richard!" Selina saw no reason now to show restraint. She turned within his embrace and threw her arms about his neck.

All her many years of worry were ended, though she

could not fully grasp yet the enormity of that fact. Augustus, who had been her companion, her brother, and her child—all the world to her—would at last get a part, a very large part, of what he deserved.

Which was what made it difficult, a few minutes later, for Selina to express her remaining dissatisfaction.

"It does seem unfair," she ventured, distracted by the tickle of Richard's lips near her ear, "that Wilfrid should come out of this at all a winner. So grossly unfair—are you sure there is nothing you might do to keep him from inheriting?"

"Well . . ." Richard held himself away, and a calculating smile touched his lips. "There might be one thing I could do, but I would need your assistance."

"Anything, Richard," she exclaimed eagerly, bouncing up in his arms. "Do you mean to call him out, for I'm sure he deserves it, though"—a thought came to her—"of course, I would not want any harm to come to you." She frowned. "But I do not think he has the look of a gentleman who would know how to fight well, do you? Perhaps you could force him to call you out, so the choice of weapons would be yours? I realize there might be consequences of the law to be dealt with, but if you ran him through with your sword, I could be right on the spot with a carriage and we could—"

"Flee for the Channel?" Richard laughed unrestrainedly. "I might have known you would think of a violent solution." He gave her his deepest grin. "But that was not precisely what I had in mind."

"No?" Selina was ashamed to feel disappointment. If it were her place, she would call Wilfrid out in an instant; but he was Richard's cousin, and Richard had a right to solve this his own way.

"No. I was thinking of something much more pleasurable."

The sudden heat in his voice warmed her long before she understood. A curious leap of her heart made her raise her eyes to his.

Richard gazed back at her like a starving man who's been lingering outside a banquet hall for too long.

"You said you would do anything?" he said, bringing his lips closer to hers.

Selina gulped and promised, "Yes, Richard, I would."

"Then, we must see how quickly we can be married and how many little Trevelyans we can place in Wilfrid's way."

The simple solution struck her, and her own foolishness for not seeing it made her laugh just as Richard covered her mouth with his. Selina discovered just how much a kiss could improve upon the thrill of laughter.

When Richard had quite drunk his fill of her for the moment, and they both had surfaced, breathing roughly, he said, "I hope that laugh did not mean you are refusing me your aid?"

"Not at all," she assured him, smiling like a contented cat and winding both her arms about his neck. "If I can be of any help to you in this respect, you only have to ask. No task is too daunting for me."

come"—he began to usher her from the room—